EASY BAIT

"You always say what is on your mind—is that how it is?"

"The missionaries told us to tell the truth and nothing but the truth," Kean answered. "To do otherwise is a sin."

"Those sins make handy excuses, don't they?"

Keanuenueokalani sat back, her luscious mouth puckered. "I am not so sure I like you anymore."

Fargo was about to say that he did not care whether she did or she didn't. All he wanted was for her to be honest with him, which she had not been so far. But then a shadow fell across their table and a great booming rumble like that of a bear in a cave put an end to their spat.

"Did you think I wouldn't find you, girl?"

Kean gave a start and nearly dropped her drink. "No! Go away! Leave me be!"

Fargo looked up to find a human walrus in seaman's garb with his big hands on his hips. "Let me guess. You would be Captain Theodore Strang."

"That I am, landlubber. And you are Keanuenueokalani's protector, I hear. But someone should have warned you," the walrus growled. "Going up against me is the same as asking for an early grave."

THE TRAILSMAN

#312

SHANGHAIED SIX-GUNS

by

Jon Sharpe

A SIGNET BOOK

SIGNET
Published by New American Library, a division of
Penguin Group (USA) Inc., 375 Hudson Street,
New York, New York 10014, USA
Penguin Group (Canada), 90 Eglinton Avenue East, Suite 700, Toronto,
Ontario M4P 2Y3, Canada (a division of Pearson Penguin Canada Inc.)
Penguin Books Ltd., 80 Strand, London WC2R 0RL, England
Penguin Ireland, 25 St. Stephen's Green, Dublin 2,
Ireland (a division of Penguin Books Ltd.)
Penguin Group (Australia), 250 Camberwell Road, Camberwell, Victoria 3124,
Australia (a division of Pearson Australia Group Pty. Ltd.)
Penguin Books India Pvt. Ltd., 11 Community Centre, Panchsheel Park,
New Delhi - 110 017, India
Penguin Group (NZ), 67 Apollo Drive, Rosedale, North Shore 0745,
Auckland, New Zealand (a division of Pearson New Zealand Ltd.)
Penguin Books (South Africa) (Pty.) Ltd., 24 Sturdee Avenue,
Rosebank, Johannesburg 2196, South Africa

Penguin Books Ltd., Registered Offices:
80 Strand, London WC2R 0RL, England

First published by Signet, an imprint of New American Library,
a division of Penguin Group (USA) Inc.

First Printing, October 2007
10   9   8   7   6   5   4   3   2   1

The first chapter of this book previously appeared in *Idaho Impact*, the three
hundred eleventh volume in this series.

Copyright © Penguin Group (USA) Inc., 2007
All rights reserved

 REGISTERED TRADEMARK—MARCA REGISTRADA

The Trailsman

Beginnings . . . they bend the tree and they mark the man. Skye Fargo was born when he was eighteen. Terror was his midwife, vengeance his first cry. Killing spawned Skye Fargo, ruthless, cold-blooded murder. Out of the acrid smoke of gunpowder still hanging in the air, he rose, cried out a promise never forgotten.

The Trailsman they began to call him all across the West: searcher, scout, hunter, the man who could see where others only looked, his skills for hire but not his soul, the man who lived each day to the fullest, yet trailed each tomorrow. Skye Fargo, the Trailsman, the seeker who could take the wildness of a land and the wanting of a woman and make them his own.

The Kingdom of Hawaii, 1861—a Garden of Eden, but every Eden has its serpent.

1

The trouble started over a woman. It often did.

Skye Fargo was having a grand time making the rounds of the saloons and taverns along the San Francisco waterfront. His poke bulged at the seams, thanks to a lucky night at monte. Usually poker was his poison, but in San Francisco, monte was more popular, and on a whim, he had tried his hand at it and won big. Now he was treating himself to a few days of whiskey and sultry doves before he headed for Wyoming.

It was nice to relax, nice not to have to worry about hostiles out to lift his hair or outlaws after his money, or to wonder whether a hungry griz was over the next rise or a rattler was in his blankets in the morning.

As for gambling and pleasures of the flesh, neither New Orleans nor Denver could hold a candle to San Francisco. The city was only slightly tamer than during its heyday of the gold rush years when, by one newspaper's estimate, there had been more than five hundred saloons and taverns and almost a thousand gambling dens. Sinner's Heaven, some called it, and the nickname fit. A man could buy most anything and do most anything. The only vices frowned upon were murder and rape. At one time San Francisco had a murder a night, or more—a statistic the vigilantes put a stop to by inviting those who indulged to be guests of honor at a hemp social.

San Francisco was growing up. During the day it was as respectable as any other city. But at night the lust and greed crept out of the shadows and ruled the streets and alleys until the next dawn.

It was pushing midnight when Fargo came to a seedy section of the docks and a tavern that sat off by itself near the water's edge. He almost passed the place by, but the gruff laughter and bawdy oaths that wafted from an open window, to say nothing of a particularly pleasing female voice, persuaded him to give the place a try.

Fargo paused with his hand on the latch and gazed out over the benighted bay. The water was black as pitch except for where shore lights were mirrored by the still surface. The smell of salt water and fish was strong.

Ships choked the shoreline with so many masts that, in the daytime, it lent the illusion of being a forest of firs. Many of the vessels, Fargo had been told, were abandoned gold rush derelicts being converted to landfill as the city spread and prospered.

The hinges rasped as the door swung in. A cloud of cigar and pipe smoke wreathed Fargo. So did odors a lot less pleasant than that of the sea.

The tavern was called the Golden Gate but there was nothing golden about it. The place was as shabby and squalid an establishment as any Fargo had ever set eyes on. Lamps were few and the lighting poor, which was just as well. The floor had not been swept in a coon's age. The walls were grimy, the bar speckled with stains. So were the glasses the bartender filled and passed to customers, but no one seemed to mind.

The tavern was packed. Townsmen in high derby hats rubbed elbows with sailors and Chinese and clean-shaven patrons of Spanish extraction who wore wide-brimmed sombreros and long serapes. Here and there were women in tight dresses with ready smiles.

One of those women attached herself to Fargo as he threaded toward the bar. A warm arm looped around his and a tantalizing violet scent eclipsed all the others. Fargo glanced into a pair of lovely eyes the same shade of blue as his. "Do you want something?" he asked with a grin.

"The name is Molly." She had curly brown hair and full lips and the tired air of a person who had seen it all and done it all, too. "Buy me a drink and I will keep you company."

"You had your choice of any gent in the place and you picked me?" Fargo mentioned.

"Your clothes made me curious," Molly said, plucking at one of the whangs on his sleeve. "We don't get many like you in here."

Fargo grunted. She was referring to his buckskins. His white hat, brown with dust, and his red bandanna and boots were ordinary enough, but buckskins were the mark of a frontiersman, and few of those ever visited San Francisco.

"Don't get me wrong. There is nothing wrong with wearing deer hide. Hell, I don't care what a man wears so long as he is friendly and treats me nice."

"I am and I will," Fargo assured her, and sliding his arm around her slender waist, he contrived to run his hand across her bottom.

"Oh, my." Molly grinned. "Aren't you the frisky devil? But no pawing until you buy us each a drink. Otherwise I might get in trouble."

"Oh?"

"My boss doesn't like us girls to give it away for free," Molly explained. "He can be a tyrant when it comes to money."

Fargo shouldered between a pair of seamen and gave the bar a thump. "Bartender! A bottle of your best."

"You'll spoil me, handsome," Molly teased. "I'm used to the cheap stuff."

"This is just a start," Fargo said as the bottle and two dirty glasses were produced. "Later on I might treat you to a meal."

"Well, aren't you the perfect gentleman?" Molly bantered. "But Mrs. McGreagor's daughter is not one to be looking a gift horse in the mouth. Whenever you have a hankering to belly up to the feed trough, I will be honored to accompany you."

Fargo filled their glasses. He raised his and she raised hers and they clinked them together. "To your health, Molly McGreagor."

"To handsome devils in buckskins," Molly responded, and tossed her drink down with a gulp. When Fargo arched an eyebrow, she chuckled lustily. "I've had a lot of practice."

Motioning at their surroundings, Fargo asked, "Why this dive? You're pretty. You're bright. You could work most anywhere."

"What a kind thing to say," Molly said. "But the truth of it is, I have a temper. I have been in a few scrapes, pulled a knife a time or three, and none of the better establishments will have me."

"You don't aim to pull a knife on me, do you?" Fargo inquired, only partly in jest. Some doves were too temperamental for their own good. That, and hard drink, made them downright dangerous.

Molly laughed and touched his cheek. "Not unless you give me cause."

"Which would be what?" Fargo wanted to learn.

"I won't have a hand laid on me," Molly recited. "I won't be kicked. I won't do things I don't want to do, and I expect an honest dollar for honest labor." She grinned and winked. "If you can call what I do for a living work."

Fargo decided he liked her. "Then you can rest easy. I don't beat women." The only exceptions had been females trying to kill him.

"Not all men are so considerate," Molly said. "Some are beasts. Oh, they smile and treat a girl nice until they get her in the bedroom. But once the door is locked and the shades are down, they turn into brutes. I have a friend by the name of Claire who had all her teeth knocked out. Another friend had her cheek cut and is scarred for life." Molly grew serious and grim. "That's not for me, thank you very much. I have too much pride to let anyone abuse me."

Fargo refilled her glass.

"If you ask me, there is too much wickedness in the

world," Molly declared. "The older I get, the more it bothers me. Silly, I suppose, but a person can't help how they feel." She nudged his arm. "How about you?"

"I feel like getting you under the sheets," Fargo said.

Molly blinked, then laughed. Upending her glass, she drained it and smacked it down on the bar. "Point taken. I apologize. I am here to show you a good time, not to prattle on so."

Before Fargo could tell her that was not what he meant, he was jostled from behind by a blow so hard he was knocked against the bar and made to spill some of his drink. As he started to turn, a man bellowed in anger.

"Consarn it! Watch where you're goin', missy! You damn near made me drop my grog!"

Fargo was not the only man who had been bumped. Two others were straightening and a third dripped with spilled liquor. What made it all the more remarkable was the party responsible.

It was a woman. Not much more than five feet tall, she was hidden in the folds of a woolen cloak and hood. Only her lustrous raven hair was visible, spilling as it did from the hood. The cloak was too long and dragged on the floor; plainly it was not hers but belonged to someone bigger. She looked up at them, her face lost in the folds of the hood, and said in oddly accented English, "I am sorry. I did not mean to disturb you."

The townsman with the liquor on his clothes was not satisfied. "What you meant be hanged, girl! My glass was practically full! You owe me the price of a drink."

The woman in the cloak did not say anything. Her hood swiveled toward the entrance and back again.

"Didn't you hear me?" the townsman demanded. "You owe me. Pay up." He held out his hand.

"I do not have money," the black-haired mystery woman said. "Again, I am very sorry." She sounded sincere.

"Sorry doesn't wet my throat." The townsman, a broomstick in a bowler hat, grabbed her arm.

Fargo was set to intervene but Molly beat him to it.

5

"You heard the girl, Stanley. Let her go. Accidents happen."

"Stay out of this, Molly," Stanley snapped. "You're not the one whose clothes need washing."

"Since when do you make a fuss over a little spilled red-eye?" Molly demanded. "When you are in your cups, you can't hardly hold your drinks steady."

Stanley was not amused. "All I am saying is this girl owes me for what she made me spill. She must make good."

The woman in the cloak tried to pull free. "I have already told you I do not have money."

"Then maybe you can repay me in another way." Leering, Stanley pulled her close and tried to push her hood back, but she slapped his wrist away. "Here now, girl! None of that. You're about to make me mad."

Molly stepped past Fargo and pried at the man's long fingers. "Pretend you have manners, Stan, and release her."

Without warning, Stanley gave Molly a shove that sent her stumbling against Fargo. "Enough of this! I won't have a saloon tart tell me what I should and should not do."

Flushing with anger, Molly raised her hand to slap him. Fargo made no attempt to stop her. He was half tempted to slug the jackass himself.

But just then a pair of sailors shouldered through the press of patrons and halted on either side of the woman in the cloak. One of the sailors was tall and lanky, the other of medium height and as broad as a brick wall. They ignored Stanley and Molly. Seizing the mystery woman's wrist, the tall sailor said, "We've caught up to you at last, little one. You thought you were clever but here we are."

Their quarry had stiffened and gasped. She sought to pull free but the tall sailor would not let go.

"No, you don't. We had to chase you all over creation and you are not getting away as easy as that."

"Let's cart her back," said the human wall. "The captain is mad enough and will only get madder the longer we take."

Fargo was as surprised as Molly, who stood with her luscious mouth gaping wide. Not so Stanley, who placed a hand on the tall sailor's shoulder and said, "Hold on there, friend. If this woman is a friend of yours, she owes me for a drink."

"What are you babbling about? Unhand me," the tall sailor said, and cuffed the townsman across the face.

Stanley staggered against the bar, his glass shattering on the floorboards at his feet. Everyone within ten feet heard the crack of the slap and stopped whatever they were doing to turn and stare. Fights, which were all too common in dives like this, were a prime source of entertainment.

The sailors went to leave. The tall one started to haul the woman in the cloak after him, but Stanley howled in outrage and darted around in front of them.

"Not so fast, damn your bones! You can't go around slapping people and get away with it."

Fargo wanted no part of their squabble. He was there for a good time and only a good time. He was curious about the woman in the cloak but that was as far as his interest went. Then the woman wrenched loose of the tall sailor and clutched at his buckskins.

"Please help me," she pleaded, her features lost in the folds of her hood. "They are holding me against my will."

"None of that, bitch," the tall sailor said. "Cause us trouble and the captain will take a switch to you." He snatched at her cloak.

She ducked and his fingers snagged her hood. Out spilled her luxurious mane of thick black hair, framing an exotic oval face with beautiful dark eyes. Fear and an eloquent appeal were in those eyes.

"Oh, hell," Fargo said. He unleashed an uppercut that caught the tall sailor on the point of his chin and crumpled him like so much paper.

Stanley picked that moment to take a swing at the

7

other sailor. He missed. The sailor then threw a punch at Stanley and hit another man, instead, who fell against others. The next moment it seemed like everyone was pushing and shoving and cursing and swinging.

Molly leaned toward Fargo and yelled in his ear, "We have to get her out of here!" She pushed him toward the end of the bar and a side door he had not noticed. "That way!" Taking the other woman's hand, Molly led the way, staying close to the bar, which most of the men had abandoned to take gleeful part in the brawl.

Fargo did not need prompting. The last thing he wanted was to be caught up in a tavern fight. If things got out of hand, the city police were bound to show up, and they were notorious for busting heads and sorting out the culprits later. But he had only taken a couple of steps when a rough hand fell on his shoulder and he was spun around.

"Hand the girl over!" the muscular sailor snarled as he brandished a knife.

2

Fargo did not draw his Colt. He was fast enough to unlimber it and put two slugs into the sailor before the man could stab him, but the lead might pass clean through and hit others. Instead, Fargo sprang back, and when the sailor came after him, he swept a bottle from the bar and smashed it over the man's blunt head.

For most, that would be enough to drop them where they stood. But the sailor only stopped and swore, then raised his other arm to wipe his sleeve across his dripping wet face.

Which was all the opening Fargo needed. He planted his right boot where it would hurt any man the most, and when the sailor doubled over in agony, crashed a second bottle down on the top of the man's head.

The bedlam had spread. Nearly everyone there was involved in the fracas, either slugging it out toe-to-toe or cheering on those who were doing the slugging.

Fargo avoided a bloodied pair who were trading as many oaths as blows and skirted an upended table.

Molly and the exotic woman in the cloak were waiting. The woman had pulled the hood up, hiding her face again. Molly had the side door open and beckoned for him to hurry.

Fargo dodged a thrown chair, evaded a kick by a man so drunk he could barely stand, and then was past the last of the battlers. He followed the women out into the night and slammed the door behind them. "Where to?" he asked Molly. She knew the area better than he did.

"My place. It isn't far."

The streets were dark and narrow. Many of the buildings were two- and three-story brick affairs, a symbol of San Francisco's affluence. The gold rush of forty-nine had turned the quiet little hamlet into a burgeoning metropolis. Before the gold strike, Yerba Buena, as it had been known, boasted four hundred souls. Now the renamed San Francisco burst at the seams with over sixty thousand inhabitants, with more pouring in every day.

Fargo had never heard tell of a city growing so fast. The gold was the reason. It brought by the many thousands the greedy and the hopeful—deluded sorts who thought all they had to do was stick a shovel in the ground or a pan in a stream and they would be rich. True, a lot of them did make sizable strikes, but the great majority did not. Not at the gold fields, at any rate. The business boom made more millionaires than the gold that caused the boom.

The gold also spawned pleasures galore. Every vice imaginable was to be had for the right price. Churchgoers complained that San Francisco had become Sodom and Gomorrah rolled into one, and they were not far off the mark. It was Sodom and Gomorrah, all right, but twice compounded. No other city in America, no other city on the continent, offered as many pursuits branded as sinful most everywhere else. A smorgasbord of illicit delights was just waiting to be savored.

All this filtered through Fargo's thoughts as he trailed the women up one street and down another. He glanced back now and again but no one was after them. Nor did any of the pedestrians they passed give them a second look.

The woman in the cloak kept her head bowed, as if afraid of being recognized.

Molly's apartment house was one of the popular prefabricated two-story wood buildings made in the East and sent around the Cape to be assembled on the spot. They reached her room by climbing a flight of stairs on the side and then quietly moving down a hall to her door. Her key rattled, and they were safely inside.

"Stand still a moment so you don't bump into anything, and I'll light the lamp."

Fargo's shoulder brushed the other woman's cloak. Her hair gave off a tantalizing scent he could not quite place. She did not look at him when the room flared with light, but kept her chin tucked.

Molly smiled and patted a chair. "Why don't you have a seat, dearie, and you can tell us what that was all about?"

"Thank you," the woman said. She sat down stiffly, gingerly, almost as if she feared the chair would break under her weight, which was ridiculous, since she must have weighed little more than a feather.

Molly turned to a cabinet and took out a whiskey bottle. She introduced herself. "What might your name be?"

"Keanuenueokalani."

In the act of opening a cupboard, Molly glanced over her shoulder. "God in heaven. What was that again?"

"Keanuenueokalani. In English it means rainbow. Most *haole*—" She stopped. "Sorry. Most whites have a hard time saying it. You may call me Kean if you wish."

"Kean it is, then." Molly brought glasses and set them on the table. "Your English is quite good, by the way, but you sure aren't American, are you?"

"No. I learned from the missionaries," Kean said. "They say I was one of their best pupils."

"Did they also tell you to wear a cloak and hood indoors?" Molly asked with a grin.

Kean pushed the hood back and gave her head a toss to free her rich, dark mane of shimmering black hair. "Again I am sorry. My manners are not what they should be."

"Where do you come from?"

"From the Kingdom of Hawaii," Kean revealed. For the first time she looked at Fargo. "I am stranded with no friends and no way of returning to those who care for me."

"That's not entirely true, sweetheart," Molly said while pouring. "You have two friends now. Handsome

11

there, and me. Why don't you tell us all about it?" Molly offered a half-full glass to her.

"I am sorry," Kean said. "I do not drink strong spirits. The missionaries said it was a sin."

Molly laughed then, and shrugged. "Suit yourself. Nearly everything I do is considered sinful, but I'll be damned if I will stop being me to suit someone else's notion of what is proper and what isn't."

Fargo was trying to recollect all he knew about Hawaii, which wasn't much. They were a bunch of islands ruled by a king. He vaguely remembered there had been a squabble a while back over religion. Protestant and Roman Catholic missionaries had been at odds over who should convert the natives. The Hawaiians picked the Protestant religion as their one and only, and threw the Roman Catholics into prison. That upset France, which blockaded the main port until the Hawaiians gave in and permitted Roman Catholic priests to go on fighting for their souls.

Kean was staring at him. "I was brought to your country by Captain Theodore Strang. Do you know of him?"

Fargo shook his head.

"I do," Molly said. "A whaler, unless I am mistaken. Some of his men have been in the tavern but I've never seen him personally." She tapped the table, her brow knit. "Doesn't Strang have a ship called the *Poseidon*?"

"That is the one, yes. A wicked man," Keanuenueokalani said, and trembled as if she were cold. "He came to our village. He told my father he wanted me, and when I would not go, Captain Strang came in the middle of the night and had his men seize me and wrap me in a blanket and carry me off."

"Wait a minute," Molly said. "The bastard took you against your will? Stole you right out of your home?"

Sadness overcoming her, Kean nodded. "From our hut."

"That's not right, and I'm pretty damn sure it's not legal, either," Molly said.

"Captain Strang does not care," Kean said. "He boasted to me that he can do as he pleases. He is white and I am not, and that means I am his to do with as he desires."

Fargo had run up against that attitude before. A lot of whites deemed it their right to treat the red man any way they wanted. That included wiping the red man from the face of the earth.

"Hell to that," Molly snapped. "Strang can't own you like he would a dog. You should talk to someone. Have the son of a bitch arrested."

"Talk to who?" Keanuenueokalani asked.

Molly turned to Fargo. "We can take her to the police but I doubt they have—what do you call it?—jurisdiction."

"A lawyer might know what to do," Fargo suggested.

"They cost money, and I'm not exactly rolling in cash and coin," Molly said.

Fargo touched his shirt. His poke was under it, suspended from a rawhide thong around his neck. "I might be able to help."

Kean, excited, started to come out of her chair, but sat back down and politely asked, "You would do that for me? A person you have just met? What do you expect in return?"

Molly answered before Fargo could. "In this country we have a saying. 'Don't look a gift horse in the mouth.' If handsome here cares to lend you a hand, take him up on it. Or don't you want to see your loved ones again?"

Kean grew sad. "I want to see them very much. My mother, my father, my four sisters and six brothers—I miss them all."

"Dear God!" Molly exclaimed. "They believe in big families where you come from."

"I live on an island called Oahu. Our village is close to a lagoon south of the Koolau Range."

"What strange names you people use," Molly said. "But suppose we wait to figure out what we are going to do with you until morning. I only have one bedroom and the one bed. You are welcome to sleep on the settee, but it won't be all that comfortable."

"I will sleep on the floor," Keanuenueokalani said.

"Like hell you will," Molly responded, and patted Kean on the shoulder. "We can settle the sleeping arrangements later. I have to get back to the tavern. The brawl should be over by now." She walked over to Fargo and touched his cheek. "Handsome here will watch over you until I get back."

"What?" Fargo said. He would rather go to the tavern with Molly and catch up on his drinking.

"Someone has to. Since I don't get off until midnight, you're elected." Molly smiled sweetly at him and then at the young Hawaiian woman, and was out the door before either of them could object.

"A remarkable woman," Kean said. "I like her."

"She's a little too bossy," Fargo grumped. Aware the Hawaiian girl was watching him, he stepped to the table, filled a glass, and swallowed the contents at a gulp. The whiskey burned clear down to his stomach.

"Forgive me for being so bold, but you do not appear happy to be with me."

"It's not that," Fargo said. But it was. Playing nursemaid was not on his list of ways to spend the next several days.

"You can leave if you are uncomfortable," Kean said. "I will be all right here by myself. Captain Strang does not know where I am."

Fargo thought of the two sailors at the tavern. On an impulse he moved to the window and peered out without showing himself. The street below was dark and empty. He was about to turn away when a pinpoint of light gleamed in a doorway on the other side of the street.

A man was lighting a pipe, his face upturned to their window.

Fargo quickly drew back.

"What is it?" Kean inquired.

Fargo told himself he must be mistaken. No one had followed them. But when he peered out again after a minute, wisps of smoke curled from the doorway. The man was still there.

"Please. You have seen something?"

Fargo told her.

14

"I knew Theodore would not give up," Kean said. Crestfallen, she placed her face in her hands. "What have I done to deserve this? How have I offended the great God?"

"What are you talking about?"

"I am being punished for a sin, but I do not know what the sin is," Kean said forlornly. "I have tried to live pure in spirit as the missionaries would have me live. Where did I fail?"

Fargo had a more urgent concern. The sailor at the tavern had been willing to knife him to get to her. "How bad does this Strang want you?"

"He would kill to keep me. He has told me so."

"We're getting out of here," Fargo said. Crossing to the chair, he grabbed her hand. She didn't protest as he pulled her to the door. Cracking it open, he peered out. The hallway was deserted. "Stay close to me," he whispered.

"Be careful," Keanuenueokalani whispered. "Wicked men work for Captain Strang. There are Berm and Gliss and—"

"Tell me about them later." Fargo slipped out and shut the door after them. His hand on his Colt, he glided to the end of the hall. The door to the stairs was ajar. Molly might have left it open when she left, but somehow he doubted it. Letting go of Kean, he put a finger to his lips. Then, lowering his shoulder, he slammed into the door.

The sailor on the landing was caught flat-footed. Flung against the rail, he clawed at a revolver wedged under his belt.

Instantly, Fargo stooped, grabbed the man's ankles, and heaved. He was rewarded with a shriek as the sailor went over the rail. Whirling, Fargo started down the steps, taking three at a bound. He was halfway down when two shadows separated from the night and moved to bar his way. Both were sailors. Both had revolvers.

Fargo was quicker. He drew his Colt and fired two swift shots, one for each. He was not trying to kill, but he was not trying not to kill, either. They collapsed, and a few more bounds brought him to the bottom. He turned to make sure Kean had done as he told her and was pleased to find her a step behind. Gripping her hand, he veered to the right, across a patch of grass to a slat fence. A gate opened on an alley.

Fargo ran, grateful for the dark. Shouts warned him of pursuers, coming from all directions. There had to be a half dozen or more, leading him to wonder just what in hell he had gotten himself into.

Just then a pistol belched lead and flame almost in his face.

3

That the shot missed was not the fault of the shooter.

Fargo glanced back at a shout from behind them, and the slug that would have cored his temple missed his head by a whisker. As it was, the blast was so close to his left ear that his inner ear flared with pain and for a brief span he could not hear out of it. By then he had spun and shot the sailor responsible, gripped Keanuenueokalani's wrist, and raced to the end of the alley.

Somewhere a bell pealed. It was a signal the police used.

Fargo guessed he had maybe five minutes before the minions of the law arrived. They frowned on the discharge of firearms within the city limits. They frowned even more on shooting a man down, and so far he had three to his tally.

Kean did not say a word as Fargo sprinted to an intersection and turned, heading away from the bay. He sensed she was relying on him to see her through, and he was not entirely comfortable with her trust. They hardly knew one another.

"This way!"

Fargo ran faster. He had always been fleet of foot and he called on that fleetness now. To his surprise, Kean not only kept up with him, she was not winded by the pace he was setting. He sensed she could run faster so he pushed himself to his limit. She stayed right with him, running smoothly and breathing easily. Whatever else she might be, Fargo reflected, she was no city girl. Her

17

long, effortless strides hinted at a life in the wild, or at the very least, a life that had hardened her muscles to an exceptional degree.

They turned right, and they turned left, never the same way twice, intersection after intersection, until the sounds of pursuit faded.

At last Fargo darted down into a stoop and stood in the inky blackness listening for footfalls.

Keanuenueokalani's hand found his arm. "Do you think we have lost them?" she whispered.

"Maybe," was all Fargo would concede. He thought he had lost them after the tavern.

"You run like a deer."

"So do you."

"In my own land I go everywhere on foot," Kean said. "My people are good runners. It pleases me that you are, too."

Fargo did not see what that had to do with anything.

"Do you know where we are? To me this city is a maze. I become easily lost. It is not like my island, where I know every path and trail."

"We can't be far from the center of the city," Fargo guessed. "There will be lots of people. We should be safe." He didn't believe it for a second but she might.

"I will do whatever you want."

There it was again, that trust. Fargo glanced at her, but all he could see in the dark was the slightly lighter oval of her face. "We'll wait here awhile to be sure."

"To be sure," she echoed.

Fargo rose onto the tips of his toes and scanned the block. A few townspeople were all he saw. He stepped back and bumped into Kean, feeling the contours of her firm breasts on his back. "I didn't mean to do that."

"To do what?" Kean asked, and then, "Oh. It is all right. I am not offended, even if it was a sin."

"I don't know as that qualifies," Fargo said.

"The missionaries have taught my people that for a man to touch a woman or a woman to touch a man is sinful. Until they opened our eyes, we foolishly believed it was natural and normal."

18

"I've always believed it was," Fargo said without thinking.

"How can it be natural and a sin at the same time?" Keanuenueokalani asked.

"If I had the answer to that I would be pounding a pulpit for a living," Fargo said.

"In my grandmother's time, women were free to do as they pleased with men. They swam out to the great ships and spent nights with any man they liked. Then the missionaries came. They said it was wicked and put a stop to it. In my mother's time more sins were added. In my time we are taught that touching is permitted only between a husband and a wife. In my daughter's time, if ever I have a daughter, they will probably say even that is a sin. Then no one will touch, and no more babies will be born, and that will be that."

Fargo was so intent on the street that he was slow to appreciate her humor. Chuckling, he turned and whispered, "You have an interesting way of putting things."

"Everyone says I think too much. It is my curse."

"Does Captain Strang say the same?"

"He has no interest in a woman's mind. Only in her body. In mine, in particular." Her bluntness was refreshing.

"Out of all the women in Hawaii, why you?" Fargo was curious to find out.

Keanuenueokalani hesitated. "Captain Strang saw me once when I came to Honolulu with my father. He decided he wanted me, and had his men take me against my will. Here I am."

Fargo had a hunch there was more to her tale. A lot more. "Love at first sight—is that how it was?"

"Lust at first sight," Kean amended. "He wants me for his own but I have refused to give in."

"Are you saying he hasn't laid a hand on you? He brought you all the way from Hawaii and never once forced himself on you?"

"If he did he knows I would hate him forever," Kean declared. "He could not bear my hate so he leaves me be."

Fargo was puzzled. Something was not adding up. She had made it sound as if Theodore Strang was a vile brute who had torn her from her family and her home to have his way with her—only he had not laid a hand on her. Fargo had several questions he wanted to ask, but just then a shoe scraped the street near the stoop and he glanced up to see two sailors hurry past. Whether they were from the *Poseidon* or another ship he couldn't say, but he covered them with the Colt until they were out of sight.

Kean edged closer. Her arm was against his; her hand brushed his leg. "Are they gone?"

"Yes," Fargo answered. "Did you recognize them?"

"I never saw those two before. But there are dozens on Captain Strang's ship and he kept me below most of the voyage." Kean's warm breath tickled his neck. "We must treat every seaman as an enemy."

Fargo bit off a reply. The notion was ridiculous. On any given day of the week there were hundreds of sailors in San Francisco. As if to confirm it, he spied a half dozen more across the street. Pulling Kean down beside him, he hunkered. Neither spoke until the sailors' footfalls faded. Then she cleared her throat and whispered, "I have not thanked you yet for what you are doing for me. Permit me to do so now."

In the confines of the stoop, the flowery fragrance of her hair was stronger than ever. It was all Fargo could do not to reach out and run his fingers through it.

"I trust you will not think it bold of me, but Molly McGreagor was right," Keanuenueokalani whispered. "You are handsome. Most handsome indeed."

Fargo wondered what she was playing at. "Keep your mind on Strang and his men," he cautioned. But he was a fine one to talk. His gaze strayed to the swell of her bosom. A familiar hunger came over him but he refused to give it rein. Rising, he warily climbed the steps to the street and looked both ways. Not a sailor was in sight. "Come on."

"Is there somewhere special you are taking me?"

Fargo was heading for Portsmouth Square. Legend

had it that back when San Francisco was known as Yerba Buena, the square had been a potato patch. Now it was the city's cultural hub. The best of everything bordered it: the most fashionable saloons, the most expensive hotels, the finest of the gambling halls, the highest-priced restaurants. Since many were open twenty-four hours a day, Portsmouth Square was always thronged with people.

Fargo figured there would be safety in numbers. He reasoned that Strang's men would not want witnesses, or meddlers.

"Is it possible—" Keanuenueokalani began, but did not finish.

"What?" Fargo prompted.

"Is it possible we could eat? I have not had food since yesterday, and I am famished."

Fargo stopped and regarded her before asking, "Strang didn't bother to feed you?"

"I refused to eat to protest my abduction. Every few days I was forced by hunger to give in and eat a little to stay alive, but that was all."

"I know a place and it's not far." Fargo was thinking of the Occidental Restaurant. It catered to the city's prosperous and the food did not come cheap, which made it about the least likely place in all of San Francisco to find sailors. The pittances they were paid were spent in cheap taverns and gin mills, where they could get more for the little they had.

Fortunately, the Occidental did not impose a dress code. Any customer who had the money to pay for the fare was welcome. And what fare it was. Every delicacy known to man was offered. The list of meats alone was enough to make the famished drool. Duck, goose, brant, quail, clover, partridge, chicken, and turkey were but a few of the fowl. Fish included salmon and trout. Oysters were hugely popular. Beef and mutton were offered, as well as venison, elk meat, antelope, rabbit, and even juicy grizzly bear steaks. Turtle soup, for those so inclined, was the priciest item on the menu.

Fargo had only eaten there once, the last time he was

in San Francisco. A young lady of his acquaintance had insisted he take her, and since he had wanted to put her in the mood for a dalliance, he gave in and treated her, even though he about went broke. But tonight he had a full poke, so after the finely dressed waiter made a show of seating them, Fargo told Kean that she could have anything she wanted.

Keanuenueokalani had checked her cloak. Under it she had on a simple yellow dress. Fairly new, by the looks of it. The dress clung snugly, accenting her feminine charms, which were considerable. Combined with her grace and poise, it lent her an aspect of exceptional beauty few women in the restaurant—few women anywhere—could match. She had gone to the ladies' and done whatever it was women did with their hair and faces, and it was no wonder she turned virtually every male head she passed.

Fargo was mightily stirred himself. But he did not let himself think about her as he ordered a thick slab of antelope with all the trimmings. Kean chose turtle soup and salmon. She had taken him at his word that she could ask for anything she wanted.

The Occidental claimed to offer over one hundred varieties and mixes of alcohol. The waiter looked severely disappointed when all Fargo wanted was plain whiskey, but he brightened when Kean asked for a Pineapple Do, a mix of pineapple, sugar, bitters, and rum. They sipped in silence, an island of quiet in a sea of bustle and din, until Kean set down her Pineapple Do and looked him in the eyes.

"How much can I depend on you?"

"Seems to me you have depended on me a lot already," Fargo mentioned.

"True. I thanked you once and I will thank you again." Kean paused. "Now that I am free, I want more than anything to return to my people. I want more than anything to go back to Hawaii."

"I will do what I can," Fargo said. Which wasn't much. To his knowledge, none of the few sea dogs he knew were in San Francisco.

"I must be on the next ship leaving for Hawaii," Kea-nuenueokalani said.

"They don't give passage for free."

"Do you know how much it would cost? Or how I can go about acquiring the money? I would not impose on your generous nature more than I already have," Keanuenueokalani said.

Fargo had been called a lot of things but generous was not one of them. "Maybe Molly will have some ideas. I sure don't." He changed the subject. "Tell me more about Captain Strang, about why he took you."

Before she sipped her Pineapple Do, Kean gave him a frosty glance over the rim. "I have already explained. He wants me for his own."

"Wants you enough to kill to keep you."

"You are skeptical, I can tell." Kean sounded hurt. "What must I do to convince you?"

"You don't need to convince me of anything, lady," Fargo said, annoyed. "I'm just curious, is all."

"I do not enjoy being called a liar."

Fargo polished off his whiskey and motioned to the waiter for another. "You always say what is on your mind—is that how it is?"

"The missionaries told us to tell the truth and nothing but the truth," Kean answered. "To do otherwise is a sin."

"Those sins make handy excuses, don't they?"

Keanuenueokalani sat back, her luscious mouth puckered. "I am not so sure I like you anymore."

Fargo was about to say that he did not care whether she did or she didn't. All he wanted was for her to be honest with him, which she had not been so far. But then a shadow fell across their table and a great booming rumble like that of a bear in a cave put an end to their spat.

"Did you think I wouldn't find you, girl?"

Kean gave a start and nearly dropped her drink. "No! Go away! Leave me be!"

Fargo looked up to find a human walrus in seaman's

garb with his big hands on his hips. "Let me guess. You would be Captain Theodore Strang."

"That I am, landlubber. And you are Keanuenueo-kalani's protector, I hear. But someone should have warned you," the walrus growled. "Going up against me is the same as asking for an early grave."

4

Ship captains were a tough breed. They had to be. Their crews were made up of men who would as soon grumble as work. Only one thing impressed them. Only one thing kept them in line. That was toughness. A captain had to be stronger and meaner than those under him. He had to enforce his will with iron discipline. A hint of weakness, and his crew was apt to mock him behind his back and generally comport themselves as they saw fit.

Captain Theodore Strang was a model of the breed. He was wide of shoulder and thick through the chest and middle; his face bore the stamp of sun and wind. He had a perpetual squint, the result of years of sea glare, and a perpetual scowl, the result of a hard-as-steel temperament. His wide hat and broad-skirted coat and baggy pants added to the impression of size and raw physical power. He had a neatly trimmed beard and a thick mustache, and whiskers that bristled like wire wool below his temples. His jaw jutted like the prong of an anchor. His eyes were a strange hue, almost copper, with a hard glint that could intimidate the timid at a glance.

Without being invited to join them, Captain Strang slid an empty chair from a neighboring table, swung it around, and straddled it. He did it without once taking those hard, coppery eyes off Fargo. He was taking Fargo's measure and making no secret of it. "Before we get to me, let's talk some of you. A frontiersman, plainly. A son of the prairies and the mountains, as I am a son of the seven seas. You would be well advised to go back

25

to those prairies and mountains, Daniel Boone, and not stick your nose where it is not wanted."

"The name is Fargo."

"Who you are is of no consequence. Only your infernal meddling matters."

Fargo did not say anything.

"You shot three of my men tonight. One is dead and another might soon be. For that, as well as your meddling, you have brought my wrath down on your head. Blame no one but yourself for what I have in store for you."

Still Fargo did not speak.

"I could overlook your ignorance, but not your arrogance," Strang continued. "Never that. No one, no creature alive, can expect to impose on me with impunity." The walrus finally paused. "Say something, you damned smug bastard."

"Those men I shot were trying to shoot me."

"Only after you chucked one of their own over a rail. His shoulder is broke, and several ribs, besides. But that is neither here nor there. The important thing is that I could go to the police and file a complaint, and they would clap you behind bars." Captain Strang smiled. "But I won't. Can you guess why?" When Fargo did not reply, he said, "I harpoon my own whales."

All this time Keanuenueokalani had sat with her hands clasped tight, her posture that of a doe poised to take flight.

Captain Strang took notice of her. "What's this, my dear? Nary a comment? Where is that tart tongue of yours? Surely you want to lash me with it? Or have you worn it out telling your protector whatever lies you have been spoon-feeding him?"

"I hate you, Theodore," Kean said.

"Hate, my dear, is but one step from love. And you do not hate me so much as you hate the manner in which I have intruded in your life. Under the circumstances, though, I fail to see how you could expect any different."

"You are a pig."

26

"Now, now. That was juvenile. Say what you will, but you must admit I have treated you with respect. Have I laid a hand on you? Has anyone? Were my crew perfect gentlemen on the way here?" Captain Strang chuckled. "That in itself was a minor miracle. But when I give an order, they by God obey."

Fargo was perplexed. This man was not at all what he expected. It was time he got some answers. "That's what I don't savvy."

"Eh?" Strang looked at him and scowled. "You wade in at last? Perhaps you would care to elaborate."

"You take Kean against her will, to be your woman, I gather. But you don't touch her. It makes no sense."

Strang switched his scowl to Keanuenueokalani. "I was right. You have been feeding your protector lies. Or at the best, half-truths."

Kean stiffened in resentment. "Was it a lie that you took me from my family and my home against my will? Was it a lie that you brought me to your country even though I pleaded with you not to?"

"You have no honor, girl," Captain Strang declared.

Kean came out of her chair swinging. Her open palm met his cheek with a loud slap. Heads at other tables turned and the waiter came hurrying over.

"Is everything all right, madam?" the waiter asked.

Captain Strang did the last thing Fargo expected; he smiled. The slap had no more effect on him than a mosquito sting, yet she had hit him hard. His cheek bore the imprint of her hand. "Go polish a spoon or something. This is personal."

The waiter drew himself up to his full height and sniffed. "Really, sir. I must protest. The Occidental does not tolerate rude or uncouth be—"

He did not get to finish. Strang's hand shot up and grabbed the waiter by the front of his fancy jacket. The man bleated as he was jerked down so they were nose to nose.

"Do you have any notion who I am?" Strang demanded.

"N-n-n-no, sir," the waiter stuttered.

27

Strang told him. "Does that name mean anything to you?"

It clearly did. The waiter blanched and looked fit to faint. "I'm sorry. I didn't recognize you. Please forgive my ill manners."

"You're forgiven," Strang said with only slight contempt. He let go, smiled, and smoothed the man's jacket. "Now run along and tend to your other customers. If we want you, I will whistle."

Kean's mouth was curled in disgust. "Was that necessary? You humiliated that poor man."

"Not nearly as much as you humiliated me by running off," Captain Strang rejoined. "And to what end? You only postpone the inevitable. Our course is set, yours and mine. Nothing you do will change it."

"I am a free woman. I can do as I please."

Captain Strang sat back and sighed. "This whole affair would go much more smoothly if you were more like your father. He is a man of his word."

"I did not give my word," Kean said angrily.

Fargo was being ignored but that changed when he asked, "Word about what?"

Strang's scowl returned. "I forgot you were here, frontiersman. But no matter. I have explained as much as I am going to. Keanuenueokalani and I are leaving now. You will stay right where you are."

"I'm not one of your men," Fargo said. "You don't tell me what to do."

"I beg to differ," Strang said, and gestured.

Fargo shifted in his chair. Unnoticed, a half dozen seamen had come up, ringing their table. All wore knives on their hips. Several had hands under their coats, which suggested they were also armed with revolvers. Each was tensed to pounce at a command from their captain.

"I repeat," Strang said. "I am leaving with the young lady. Interfere and your time on this earth can be numbered in seconds."

Kean's eyes met Fargo's. He was sure he could draw and shoot two or three of the sailors before the others could blink, but the captain's next comment made him reconsider.

"Any innocents who are harmed will be on your shoulders."

Every table was filled. Were lead to fly, a lot of bystanders would not live to taste dessert. Fargo placed his hands flat on the table as a sign that he would not resist.

"Smart man," Captain Strang said. He rose and beckoned to Kean. "Come, my dear. All your effort has been for naught. Accept the inevitable and you will be a lot happier."

"Never," Keanuenueokalani said. But she rose and permitted him to hook his arm in hers. As they went to leave, she gazed down at Fargo in what might have been regret. "I am sorry. I thank you for trying to help. Do not feel bad that we were caught. There are many of them and only one of you."

Captain Strang had parting words, too. "This isn't over. Not by a long shot. We will meet again, and when we do, you will rue challenging me. Mark my words."

Fargo marked instead Kean's sorrow, and the smirks thrown his way by Strang's men. No sooner did they depart than the food came. He had lost a lot of his appetite but he ate anyway. The antelope was delicious. He ate staring at the turtle soup and salmon.

"I apologize for not standing up to that awful sea captain," the waiter commented as Fargo was paying. "But he has a reputation, that one. He is as mean as they come."

"I gathered as much," Fargo said. "Would you happen to know where his ship is anchored?"

"I'm afraid not. But if you ask around at the docks someone is bound to know."

Fargo was in no hurry to return to Molly's. He had hours until midnight. A long walk brought him to the top of Telegraph Hill. From there he could see the lights of the countless vessels that lined the bay. Many more were dark silhouettes. Finding the *Poseidon* would take some doing. He did not share the waiter's confidence. Sailors were a notoriously tight-lipped bunch.

The streets were generally still as Fargo wound down the hill. He thought he heard footsteps and stopped to glance back, but no one was there. He walked on, and again heard furtive steps. When he came to a corner, he darted around the building and waited for whoever was following him to appear. No one did.

Convinced he was having an attack of nerves, Fargo tried several tricks to prove it one way or the other. He ducked into a doorway. He dropped flat in the mouth of an alley. He crossed a well-lit street and then doubled back, careful to keep in the dark. In each instance the result was the same.

Fargo began to long for the wilds. Strang had been right about one thing. He *was* a child of the mountains and the plains. They were his element, as the sea was Strang's. Not the city. In the mountains no one could stalk him and get away with it.

It was not bragging to say that he had the senses of an Apache. As well he should. Few whites had spent as much time in the wild as he had. His wanderlust had taken him from Canada to Mexico, from the Mississippi River to the Pacific Ocean.

The Pacific Ocean. Fargo gazed to the west and tried not to think of Keanuenueokalani. Whatever she was involved in did not bode well for her. He reminded himself that she had not been completely honest with him. If she had, maybe things would have turned out differently.

Molly's apartment building was quiet. Whatever uproar had resulted from the shooting earlier had long since died down. He climbed to the second floor and cracked the door. The hall was empty. He was almost to Molly's room when he saw that her door was open a hand's width. A shadow flitted within.

Fargo swooped his hand to his Colt. A kick and a spring, and he was in the room with his revolver out and level.

Molly McGreagor jumped half a foot. She had been tidying up. "Land sakes! What are you trying to do? Scare me out of ten years' growth?"

"I thought you were someone else," Fargo said, self-consciously replacing the Colt in its holster.

"Where did that cute Hawaiian girl get to? Or did you take her for a moonlit stroll and lose her?" Molly teased.

"You better sit down," Fargo said, and after she did, he related everything that had happened since she left.

"I wish I had been there," Molly said at the conclusion. "I wouldn't have let Strang get his foul hands on her."

The comment stung. It showed on Fargo's face because she suddenly reached across the table and covered his hand with hers.

"That didn't come out right. You did all you could, and then some. It's a wonder the minions of the law aren't scouring the streets for you."

"Strang didn't report me," Fargo said. "He came right out and told me he wasn't filing charges."

"Peculiar, that," Molly observed. "He must have whisked the men you shot out of here before the police showed. Maybe to his ship."

"I could use a drink," Fargo said. He could use more than that but he was in no rush. He had all night. He would start searching for the *Poseidon* in the morning. Finding it at night would be next to hopeless. He must put Keanuenueokalani from his mind, as difficult as that might be.

"Sorry. Where are my manners?" Molly bounced to the cupboard and came back with the bottle and two glasses. She filled his to the brim. "To your health, handsome."

"To your body," Fargo said. The bug juice brought welcome warmth after his long walk in the chill air.

Molly grinned. Arching her spine, she thrust her bosom against her dress. "Like what you see, do you?"

"Any man would."

"If I had a dollar for every gent who has said that," Molly remarked rather wearily, but quickly brightened. "It does this gal's heart good to know she still has what it takes. I'm not as young as I used to be. In a month or so, I will turn twenty-five."

31

"That's hardly old," Fargo said.

"In my line of work, it is. They start young these days, fourteen or fifteen. The best of them, the brightest and prettiest, make enough in five or six years to quit the business and live in comfort the rest of their lives." Molly bit her lower lip, then said, "That was my plan, once. Now I only spend my time in the company of those I like, and I don't always let them get lucky."

"How is my luck?" Fargo asked.

Molly gave her hair a toss and sashayed around the table. Bending, she displayed her wares for him to admire, and winked. "Why don't you give me a go and find out?"

5

His luck proved just fine.

Molly smiled as Fargo slid out of his chair and came around the table. Her smile widened when he cupped her twin mounds and kneaded them as a baker kneaded dough. It widened even more when he pressed his hard body against her, then vanished as his mouth covered hers. Their kiss was long and languid. When it ended she was breathing heavily and her eyelids were hooded.

"That was nice. Very nice."

Fargo kissed her neck, her ear. He sucked on her earlobe, and she gripped his shoulders and cooed softly in her throat. His hands roved behind her and he squeezed her bottom. At that she ground against him, the heat between her thighs warming his loins and stiffening his manhood.

For many more minutes, they kissed and caressed, until Molly was panting with desire and Fargo felt as if he had been standing under a burning sun all day. Scooping her into his arms, he carried her to the bed and lowered her onto her back.

Playfully crooking a finger, Molly huskily urged, "Do it to me, lover. Do it to me good."

Fargo intended to. He undid his gun belt. Sitting, he removed his spurs and tugged out of his boots. When he turned to Molly, she was impatiently tapping her fingers on the quilt.

"And men say women take forever," she teased.

Fargo stretched out beside her. Again their mouths

fused. Their tongues entwined. She was soft, yielding, delicious. His hands explored her and hers explored him. Showing more signs of impatience, she hiked at his shirt. It fit so snugly he had to help her get it over his head.

Whistling in appreciation, Molly ran her palms over his whipcord abdomen. "My, oh my, treats come in buckskin packages, too, I see."

Turning her so he could get at the clasp, Fargo unfastened her dress. It took some doing. Unfortunately there were a lot of tiny buttons and hooks to contend with.

Molly had been around the barn a few times. She knew that few things frustrated a man more than wrestling with a woman's dress for a half hour. When he had pried and sworn for a few minutes, she giggled and twisted to lend a hand. Soon Fargo peeled the dress from her as he might peel a skin from a banana. She helped further by wriggling when it snagged about her hips.

Her mouth was molten, her skin hot to the touch.

Fargo freed her globes. Dipping down, he inhaled a nipple as rigid as a tack. He nipped it lightly with his teeth, eliciting a gasp of delight. He nipped the other, then lathered both breasts until they heaved with burning lust.

"I want you. I want you so damn much."

Fargo figured as much. He ran his tongue from her cleavage to her navel and swirled the tip. He licked a path to her hip and up her side to her bosom.

Molly's nails dug into his shoulders fit to shred his flesh.

He could not get enough of her firm, full breasts. He traced the outline of one and then the other. He licked and flicked her nipples. Placing a hand on each melon, he squeezed and pulled and massaged. In reaction, her hips moved of their own accord, rising off the bed to churn against his bulge.

Fargo lost track of the passage of time. He was adrift in pleasure, in a sensual narcotic as addicting as opium. He could never get enough, were he to live to be a hundred.

Presently they were naked. Chest to bosom, hip to hip, they stimulated each other, doing their best to bring the other to the summit. Their kisses became more fervent, their groping more passionate. When Fargo slid a hand between her legs to her wet slit, Molly threw back her head and groaned long and loud. He found her swollen knob and lightly feathered it with his fingertip. Her legs parted, wrapped around him, and clamped tight.

Fargo slid a finger into her and she thrust against his palm while making tiny mewing sounds. When he inserted a second finger, she grew still for a few moments, then thrust with redoubled vigor. He plunged his fingers deeper and she practically lifted him and her off the bed.

"Yes, oh yes, oh yes, oh yes."

Warm fingers enveloped Fargo's manhood. A constriction formed in his throat as she began stroking him, up and down, up and down, never too rough, never too fast, doing it just right, and in the process making him dizzy with need. He swallowed, or tried to, because his mouth had gone dry.

"Are you ready, lover? I'm ready. Please tell me you are."

Fargo let his actions answer for him. Reaching down, he aligned his member with her sheath and lightly ran the tip along her slit. Her hand closed over his, and, with a deft lift of her thighs, she impaled herself on his organ, impaled herself to the hilt. A dreamy expression came over her. Molly smiled and sighed and closed her eyes.

"This is what I live for, lover."

Fargo could understand why. Holding her hips, he commenced the rocking movement that would eventually carry them over the crest. They were a while getting there. He prolonged reaching the peak for as long as he could. By his count she had gushed twice when he finally shattered the mental dam that had contained his release.

When it was over they lay spent and exhausted. A fine sheen of sweat cooled their overheated bodies.

Gradually, Fargo drifted off. He dreamed of Keanuenueokalani. A silly dream, in which she was running along a path in a lush green valley and he was chasing her. For some reason she was naked except for a wreath of flowers around her head. She kept looking back and motioning for him to overtake her but, try as he might, he could not catch up. They ran and ran and came to the top of a high cliff and a magnificent waterfall. To his dismay, Kean ran to the edge and, without hesitation, threw herself into space. He came to the edge and stopped, out of breath. She was in the middle of a flawless dive, her arms outstretched. She looked up at him and smiled. Then she knifed into the water and was gone. He tensed to dive after her, and abruptly woke up.

Fargo lay listening. Next to him Molly breathed deeply in the rhythm of sleep. Outside her apartment a bird gaily chirped. He swiveled his head toward the window and saw a pale harbinger of impending dawn. It was too early yet to start searching for Kean so he closed his eyes and tried to get back to sleep. He couldn't. Images from the dream filtered through his mind, images so vivid he would have sworn they had really happened. After twenty minutes or so he gave it up as a lost cause.

Quietly rising, Fargo dressed and pulled his boots back on, first making sure his Arkansas toothpick was snug in its ankle sheath; then he strapped on his Colt. He could do with a cup of coffee but he did not want to wake Molly. Slipping from her apartment, he went down the hall to the outer stairs.

The eastern sky glowed pink and yellow. San Francisco was astir. Milk wagons were creaking and rattling on their morning rounds. Shopkeepers were preparing to open for the day. Wood smoke curled from the chimneys of those who could not tolerate the morning chill. Gulls wheeled and cawed out over the bay. A ship was coming into harbor, its canvas sails spread like wings.

Fargo clunked down the steps. A spattering of red drops showed where one of the seamen had fallen the night before. He made for the street and bent his steps toward the jungle of masts and vessels that choked the shore. The phrase "a needle in a haystack" came to mind, but he had to do it.

A restaurant that catered to the seafaring crowd was

doing brisk business. Perched almost at the water's edge, it had a wide window that afforded a sweeping view of the bay. Fargo ordered coffee and eggs. The woman who served him was stout and ruddy and not at all friendly. He tried her, anyway. When she brought his steaming cup, he smiled and said, "Mind if I ask you a question, madam?"

"I don't run a whorehouse, sonny, so don't call me madam. The name is Hannah. What's on your mind?"

"Have you heard of Captain Strang?"

"Heard of and heard him," Hannah said. "He comes in on occasion. A fine gentlemen, the captain. He is generous with his tips."

Fargo took that as a hint. "You wouldn't happen to know where I can find his ship, the *Poseidon*?"

"There I can't help you," Hannah said. "But the harbormaster might be able to. He keeps a log, I believe, of all the ships that come and go." Evidently she considered their talk at an end, as she took her stout self elsewhere.

Fargo waited for her to bring his eggs to ask, "Can you tell me where I can find the harbormaster?"

"At his office, where else? It is not much more than a shack but that doesn't stop him from putting on airs."

"You know him, then?"

"If by 'know' you mean in the biblical sense, then no. I am particular in that regard. But if by 'know' you mean to recognize on sight and to talk to every blue moon, then yes, he, too, stops by here to fill his belly. Floyd Barnett is the man you want. Sixtyish. A white-haired gentleman who always wears a blue cap and has a black pipe jammed in his mouth."

"This shack of his. Where would I find it?"

"Where it has always been." Hannah pointed out the window. "Follow the shoreline for a quarter of a mile. You can't miss it. There's a sign for those who can read."

Fargo thanked her and added extra when he paid. Hooking his thumbs in his gun belt, he strolled in the direction she had told him to go.

The seaport was coming alive. Crews on a legion of boats were astir. Already the smaller craft of the fishermen were making for deep water, eager to fill their nets. A tugboat was hauling a barge. Several rowboats moved among the ships, their oars dipping and rising. Of the larger vessels, a number were setting sail.

There were schooners, clippers, brigantines, and sloops. There were two-masters, three-masters, and even a few four-masters.

Sailors scrambled to obey the bellowed orders of captains and mates. Nautical slang flew fast and furious. Canvas flapped and crackled. Lines were rigged. Anchors were raised. Lookouts climbed into crow's nests.

Fargo took it all in with a fascination born of the world of difference between his world and the world of the sea. He had been on ships a few times, most recently when he ventured to Alaska, and he had to admit that life at sea held a certain appeal. He could see why some men liked it so much, why they relished the adventure and the travel and made it their life's profession. Their wanderlust was no different from his.

Several sailors were coming toward him. Crusty salts, they had the odd gait of men more accustomed to a rolling deck than solid earth under their feet. They stopped and regarded Fargo with interest when he held up a hand.

"Can you point me to the harbormaster's?"

"Past the next two ships and you'll be there," said the oldest. "But you might have to wait a bit. Floyd is not one for being punctual."

"The story goes that he'll be late for his own funeral," joked another, and all three chuckled.

Fargo thanked them and was about to move on when he felt compelled to ask, "How about the *Poseidon*? You wouldn't happen to know where I can find her?"

"Do you have business with someone on board?" the older sailor asked.

"You could say that."

"Better you than me," the sailor said. "The master of

the *Poseidon* is not the kind to welcome strangers with open arms."

"That would be Captain Strang. I thought he was highly respected," Fargo fished for information.

"So is a barracuda," the old sailor declared. "But you wouldn't catch me swimming with one."

"He can't be that bad," Fargo played the innocent.

"Mister, Captain Strang is about the meanest excuse for a human being there is," the old sailor said, and was nudged by one of his fellows.

"Keep your voice down, you bilge rat. Or do you want word to get back to him?"

The old sailor nervously glanced at the ships. "No, I wouldn't want that. Those who speak ill of Strang have a habit of having their heads busted." He looked at Fargo. "Be careful, mister, is all I'm saying. Not all sharks live in the sea, if you take my meaning."

Fargo took it, all right. He hiked on, pausing briefly to watch cargo being hoisted to a ship's hold. The shack he was seeking stood on the landward end of a long pier. A faded sign in plain black letters announced HAR-BORMASTER. He knocked and tried the door, but it was locked. He was standing there debating whether to wait or nose around when a heavyset sailor with two chins covered with stubble came ambling along the quay and out onto the jetty to the shack. He shook the door, and swore.

"Still not here? Or has he come and gone and I've missed him?"

"So far as I know he hasn't shown up yet," Fargo said.

The portly sailor swore some more and smacked the door. "Floyd missed his calling. He should be a banker, the hours he keeps. Now I have to go back and tell my captain it will be a while yet before we can leave, and he wanted to get under way before the *Poseidon*." He pivoted on a pudgy heel.

"Wait." Fargo went up to him. "Did you say the *Poseidon*?"

"She is anchored near our ship," the sailor revealed.

"They are both whalers. My captain knows her captain, and intends to raise anchor first and beat him out of the bay."

"Doesn't he like the *Poseidon*'s captain?"

The portly sailor laughed. "Oh, it's nothing like that. More in the nature of a friendly rivalry, you might say. They wager a lot. On who will get the largest whale. On who will have the nicest weather. Those sorts of things."

"Will you show me where the *Poseidon* is?" Fargo intended to find a way on board unseen and sneak Keanuenueokalani off.

"I don't see why not." The sailor headed back the way he had come, walking briskly for someone with so much extra baggage.

Fargo had to quick-step to keep up. He noticed the names of some of the ships they passed. The *Dover*. The *Rachel*. The *Pequod*. The *White Swallow*. The *Archer*. Some were clipper ships. Some were whalers. He half expected *Poseidon* to be anchored a short distance from shore, as many of the other ships were. Then the portly sailor gestured at a whaler so close in that Fargo could hit her with a rock.

"There she is, mister."

Fargo stopped. He had blundered. He did not want Strang to know he was looking for his ship, and who should be standing on the quarterdeck but Strang himself. Fargo's luck held again, though. Strang's back was to him. He started to back away and felt a sharp jab low against his spine. He glanced over his shoulder.

The portly sailor had a dagger in his hand. "And where do you think you're off to?"

6

Anger boiled in Fargo like boiling water in a pot. Not at the sailor, but at himself for being tricked. He held still as the portly sailor, chuckling, relieved him of his Colt.

"I did that slick as grease, if I do say so myself," the man praised his own cleverness. "The name is Gliss, by the way. Second mate under Captain Strang on the *Poseidon*."

Fargo remembered Keanuenueokalani mentioning the name. Something about him being wicked.

Gliss gave a loud whoop. "Captain! Look who came to pay you a visit! It worked just like you said it would!"

His hands clasped behind his back, Strang turned and gazed down at them. Tucked under his belt was a knife with a pearl hilt. "Of course it did." He bestowed a cold smile on Fargo. "I could have left last night. I could have hoisted sail and been out to sea by now. But I stayed. Can you guess why?"

Fargo did not give him the satisfaction of answering. But he could guess, and felt twice the fool.

"Bring our guest on board, Second Mate Gliss," Captain Strang commanded. "He came here to find us, so let's show him how hospitable we can be."

Other sailors had gathered and were waiting at the top of the gangplank. All had knives but none, Fargo noticed, wore pistols. Later he was to learn that Strang forbade the carrying of firearms on board. It was general policy for crews on seafaring craft as a precaution against mutiny, and against the tempers that often flared when men were cooped up on a ship for long periods.

At a poke from the dagger, Fargo held his arms out from his sides and moved toward the gangplank.

"Lower your damn hands!" Gliss snapped. "We don't want any busybodies to get curious."

Fargo complied. He had no doubt the man would bury the blade to the hilt if he tried anything. Better to go along for the moment and wait for a chance to turn the tables.

Some of the sailors were snickering and laughing. They were typical of their seafaring breed: not shaven, not very clean, their faces burned by the sun and seamed by long exposure to the wind. They were seafaring wolves, almost as tough as their captain.

Another sailor came up on deck from below. A singular individual, he was as thin as a beanpole and stood at least six and a half feet high at the shoulder. He presented quite a contrast to Gliss. A wool cap crowned a thatch of red hair that in itself was a striking contrast to his slate gray eyes. Instead of a dagger or a dirk, which many of the sea breed favored, he wore a bowie knife strapped to his skinny hip.

Fargo recognized him as the tall man he had slugged in the tavern.

"I got him, Berm," Gliss gloated anew. "It was as easy as taking pie from a child."

Another name, Fargo recollected, that Keanuenueo-kalani had mentioned. Fargo saw no trace of emotion on Berm's saturnine features.

"If it was easy," Berm said in a curiously raspy voice, "then it is nothing to brag about."

"My sentiments exactly, First Mate." The sailors parted for Captain Strang. He accepted the Colt from Gliss and hefted it in his palm. "Care to hear a story, Fargo?" he asked, and went on without waiting for a reply. "Many years ago, shortly after I first took to sea, I hired on a ship bound for the South Pacific. One day when we were at anchor near a South Seas island, some of us went for a swim. What with our cavorting, we stirred up a great devilfish. Out lashed its tail, striking one of the men in the ribs. It came for me next. But I was always a seal in the water, and when that barb slashed, I cut it off with my knife. The devilfish fled." He regarded Fargo intently. "It taught me an important lesson. Can you guess what that was?"

Fargo did not give a damn.

"It taught me that no matter how formidable an enemy is, take away their power to do you harm and they are nothing."

"So what now?" Fargo asked. "You hang me from the yardarm?"

Strang's grin was that of a cat playing with a mouse. "Heavens no. Not that you don't deserve it, after shooting my men. But where is the pleasure in killing you quickly? Retribution, as with a fine wine, should be savored slowly."

At that some of the sailors cackled. They obviously had an inkling of what lay in store.

"Kill me and you will have a murder charge over your head," Fargo stalled. All he needed was an instant's opening.

"Says the gentleman who would have one over his head were I to go to the authorities," Captain Strang rebutted. "But don't fret on that score. Murdering you is not part of my plan."

"Where is Kean?" Fargo asked.

"Never you mind about her," Strang said coldly. "She is mine, and I don't take kindly to other men showing an interest."

"She isn't yours if she doesn't want to be."

The loudest laughter yet greeted Fargo's remark. Second Mate Gliss slapped his leg and exclaimed, "Thinks he knows it all, this one! He sure has a lot to learn."

"Hush," Captain Strang said, and everyone promptly did. He extended the Colt to Berm. "Take this, First Mate, and lock it away with the rest of the guns and powder."

"Aye, aye, Captain."

Fargo's chance had come. No one had a drawn weapon

except Gliss, who was a step or two behind him. The sailors had him ringed, and there appeared to be no way he could escape. But they were mistaken.

In a blur, Fargo lunged. He snatched the Colt out of Strang's callused hand and pivoted, thumbing back the hammer as he moved, and jammed the muzzle against Strang's neck. Strang started to bring his big hands up but thought better of the idea. His men, momentarily startled, recovered and began to close in.

"No, damn your bones!" Strang roared. "Stand where you are! A twitch of his finger and I'm a dead man."

The sailors did not like it but they obeyed, several with their hands outstretched toward Fargo.

"Move back, all of you."

Only half obeyed. The rest looked to the first mate, who showed not the slightest shred of unease at the new development. "Do as he says, men," Berm instructed them. "He has us at a disadvantage."

A space was cleared, reluctantly. Fargo took the knife with the pearl hilt and cast it over the side.

After the splash, Strang cursed. "For that you will suffer double. It was a gift from my wife."

"You have a wife yet you want Kean?" Fargo asked, gouging the barrel deeper into Strang's throat.

"She died of the pox while I was at sea. Seven years ago this summer."

"Did you force yourself on her, too?"

Scarlet crept from Strang's collar to his hat. "She was a Nantucket girl, and we willingly said our vows at the altar. Besmirch her memory again and you will have to shoot me to stop me from breaking your spine over my knee."

Fargo gripped the front of Strang's coat and began to back toward the gangplank, pulling Strang after him. He alertly watched the others but they made no move to interfere, although many twitched with their eagerness to stop him. At the top of the gangplank he halted. "Bring Kean out," he said to the first mate.

Berm looked at Strang.

"No," Strang said.

"I'm not leaving without her," Fargo declared.

"You dream if you expect to take her off my ship," Strang told him. "It is not going to happen."

"Do you think I won't shoot you?"

"On the contrary," Strang said, "I am certain you will. You have killed before. I can see it in your eyes. But you won't squeeze that trigger. Because if you do, the instant I am dead, my men will rush you, and you do not have enough cartridges in your revolver to kill all of them. They will overwhelm you and use you as a pincushion."

The hell of it was, Fargo realized, the man was right.

"So let's have no talk of producing Keanuenueokalani," Strang said. "Your main concern should be leaving here alive."

Fargo agreed. He could always come back for Kean later. After the sun went down would be best. Accordingly, he slowly backed down the gangplank, careful to hold on to Strang and keep the captain between him and the crew. No one attempted to stop him, although a few took a step or two but stopped at stern words from First Mate Berm and Second Mate Gliss.

Strang acted more amused than anything else. "My men will hate you for this. They don't take kindly to being bested."

"They don't take exception to kidnapping, either."

"The girl was promised to me by her father," Captain Strang related. "I am merely collecting on a debt."

"She is a grown woman and can do as she pleases."

"You have Hawaii confused with America. The Kingdom of Hawaii does not abide by the same laws, especially in matters like this. Oh, their government has tried to keep up with the times, but many of the islanders still live by the old ways, and according to their custom, fathers may marry off their daughters as they see fit."

Preoccupied with the crew and with repeatedly glancing behind him, Fargo said, "It's not fair to the women."

Captain Strang chortled. "I did not take you for a romantic. Since when should women have a say? Hell, they don't even have the right to vote. As for the fairness of it, you must live in a different world than I do. In my world fairness does not exist. Prattling about it justifies the weak their weakness. The strong take what they want."

They were at the bottom of the gangplank. A few people on the dock had stopped what they were doing to stare.

"Order your men to stay on the ship," Fargo commanded. "You're coming with me to the harbormaster."

Strang did not hide his surprise. Or was it something else? "You are taking me to Floyd? With an aim to reporting me?" Strang perplexed Fargo by saying, "Yes. By all means. This should prove interesting."

Fargo had the seadog walk several steps in front of him. He holstered the Colt but kept his hand on it, alert for a trick.

"I must say, you intrigue me," Strang said over a wide shoulder. "That silly talk of fairness and now this. But you won't change anything. Keanuenueokalani will be my new wife, and nothing she can do, not all her shenanigans, can change that." When Fargo did not comment, Strang said with resentment he could not hide, "You would be well advised to get on with your own life and quit interfering in mine."

The door to the harbormaster's was open and from within came whistling to the tune of a popular sea shanty. Fargo told Strang to halt, then called out, "Floyd Barnett! Is that you in there?"

The man who came out was exactly as the waitress had described him: in his sixties, wearing a blue cap, and with a pipe clamped between his thin lips. His eyebrows arched when he saw Captain Strang, who smiled and nodded. To Fargo he said, "Yes, I am Barnett. Was that you who did the yelling?"

"This man is holding a woman on his ship against her will."

Barnett blinked. "What the devil are you talking about?"

Fargo repeated his statement, adding, "You're the

harbormaster. Get hold of the police and have them raid the ship."

"Raid the *Poseidon*?" Barnett turned to Strang. "What is this, Theodore? Some kind of joke? Who is this fellow?"

"It is no joke, I assure you, Floyd," Captain Strang said.

Not liking what he was hearing, Fargo asked, "Do you two know one another?"

"What a ridiculous question," Barnett said. "I have made the acquaintance of every captain on every ship in this harbor. It's part of my job."

"This one is keeping a Hawaiian woman prisoner on the *Poseidon*."

"A prisoner, you say?" Barnett scoffed. "Is this true, Theodore?"

"Judge for yourself. Just last night she was with my accuser at the Occidental Restaurant."

"Was she?" Barnett addressed Fargo.

"Yes, but—" Fargo got no further.

The harbormaster held up a hand and cut in, saying, "Enough of this nonsense. I have known Theodore Strang for almost ten years. He is one of the most widely respected captains on the seven seas. Yet you would have me take your word, the word of a complete stranger, over his. Even if your preposterous allegation is true, which I don't believe for a minute, by your own admission the woman in question is Hawaiian. A foreigner. In which case I have no authority whatsoever." Barnett made a sweeping gesture toward the bay. "I am the *harbor*master. I enforce the rules and regulations that have to do with the smooth running of this harbor. But I am not an officer of the law. For that, you must go see the police or the sheriff. Good day, sir." Without giving Fargo a chance to respond, Barnett turned and went back in, muttering irritably, "You have squandered enough of my precious time."

Captain Strang smiled. "I could have told you this would happen. What do you propose to do next?"

"Take you to the police," Fargo said.

"I think not." Strang pointed. "My men have been into the ship's armory."

Unnoticed, the first and second mates and fully a dozen members of the crew had come to within a stone's throw of the pier. Berm and Gliss had rifles. Others had revolvers.

"I can drop you before they drop me," Fargo warned.

"I don't doubt it," Strang said with mock politeness. "But they would shoot you to pieces, and where would that leave the lovely maiden you are so determined to rescue?"

In their clutches, Fargo realized. Scowling, he spun and headed for the nearest street. Several of the crew made as if to intercept him but stopped at a command from Strang.

Their laughter made Fargo's ears burn.

7

A sliver of moon hung over the bay, casting the flotilla of assorted ships with their forest of masts in a pale silver hue. The gulls were quiet, the sea lions had ceased their bellowing, and the night was as calm as the still surface of the water.

Few lights gleamed amid the host of vessels. It was two in the morning and most of the crews were abed. A few were up reading by lanterns turned low. Insomniacs were busy tidying or doing whatever else they did to tire themselves so they could sleep. Those who loved the bottle nursed a few last few sips before slumber claimed them.

On shore, a silent shadow detached itself from the corner of a building and glided toward a certain dock. The *Poseidon* was one of those vessels without lights. Everyone on board had long since turned in. But the shadow exercised utmost care. It was as wary as a mountain lion prowling the unfamiliar byways of a town or city.

Skye Fargo paused to listen and peer into the dark. The gangplank had not been taken down. That was not unusual. A lot of ships were linked by wooden umbilical cords to pier or shore. But Fargo did not go up it. He crept to the end of the pier and crouched in the ink to contemplate the ship, then uncoiled the rope he had brought. It was the work of seconds to fashion a loop.

Fargo held the rope ready to throw. The problem was, there were no projecting spars or beams on which the rope could catch. At least, none that Fargo could see. The dull glint of the anchor chain offered a possible solution. But he would have to enter the water to reach it and he did not like the thought of climbing onto the deck dripping wet. Then he saw a line, barely visible, that ran from ship to pier. He went over. It was thick enough to bear his weight and coarse enough that he would not slip. Leaving his rope on the pier, he hooked his ankles around the line and started up it hand over hand.

The deck was dark and still.

Fargo crouched by the taffrail, his senses probing. He stared long and hard at the crow's nest until he was satisfied it was empty. The absence of a lookout did not disturb him. There was no need of one.

Staying close to the rail, Fargo cautiously prowled forward. He did not like the quiet. His every instinct warned him that Strang would not be this careless, certainly not when Strang expected him to try to spirit Keanuenueokalani off the ship.

Small for her nautical breed, the *Poseidon* was a three-master. She had been built with speed in mind, and had a shallow draft. A sailor at a restaurant had told him that she was one of the swiftest whalers. *Poseidon*'s deck was over a hundred feet from stern to bow. Little else distinguished her except that her hull was darker than most, so dark as to spark comment from those who did not know that long seasons at sea had that effect, and *Poseidon* had spent more seasons at sea than most. Its smell clung to her.

Fargo made for the companionway to belowdecks. Keanuenueokalani either shared the great cabin with Strang or had a cabin of her own. There was bound to be a guard or else her door was locked. Fargo would deal with those hurdles when he came to them.

The sigh of the wind in the rigging and the creak of weathered boards were the only sounds. Fargo descended from the quarterdeck to the main deck and the companionway. Careful not to frame himself in the doorway, he peered into the passage. More odors reached him, some of them sour.

The silence of the tomb sheathed the whaler. That in itself was troubling. There should be *some* sounds. Snoring, if nothing else. But then, he did not know where the crew quarters were. Possibly farther below. He edged forward, palming his Colt.

Fargo had thought about bringing his Henry, but he had left the rifle at the boardinghouse. In the close quarters of the ship it would hamper more than help. The Colt, on the other hand, was made for situations like this.

His spurs were back at the boardinghouse, too. He made no more sound than the wind in the furled canvas.

A door appeared on the left. Fargo put his ear to it but heard nothing to give a clue to what was on the other side. Gingerly, he tried the latch. It rasped slightly and he froze. When no outcry or sleepy query resulted, he cracked the door wide enough to poke his head in.

It was a storeroom lined with shelves and stockpiled with provisions for the next voyage. It suggested the ship was ready to sail at Strang's whim.

The next door, on the right, was slightly ajar, and from within came intermittent snores. Only one person, Fargo judged. Perhaps one of the mates. He did not open the door to confirm it. Why tempt fate? It was Kean he sought.

The third door, again on the left, was locked. Fargo pressed his ear to it but heard nothing to suggest the compartment was occupied. He was about to move on when the sounds of faint scuffling reached him. He strained his ear and heard what might be the muffled sounds of someone trying to speak with a gag in their mouth.

Dropping to his hands and knees, Fargo lowered his mouth to the gap between the bottom of the door and the floor. "Kean?" he whispered. "Is that you?" He was rewarded with louder scuffling and what might have been a muffled "Yes!"

Fargo rose and glanced both ways. The passage was empty. But it would not stay empty long if he broke down the door. The alternative was to find the key, but it was bound to be in Strang's possession and he would not give it up without a fight.

Fargo pressed his shoulder to the door. The panel gave slightly under his weight. It was not as thick as a cabin or house door would be, but it was sturdy enough that his only recourse was to step back, set himself, and slam into it with all his might. To his delight it burst inward.

On a bunk against the wall lay a curled form. The person's back was to him, their legs pressed together as if their ankles were bound.

"Kean?" Fargo whispered, and sprang to free her. "I'll have you out of here in two shakes of a lamb's tail."

Fargo had to work fast. Someone was bound to have heard the door cave in. He went to untie her ankles and realized they were not bound. He realized, too, with a sickening shock, that the figure was not slender and shapely and wearing a dress, but short and broad and wearing sailor's clothes.

"Will you indeed?" Second Mate Gliss asked, and rolled over, a short-barreled pistol clutched in his thick fingers. "That's awful sweet of you, but what if I am content where I am?"

Trap! blared in Fargo's brain. "Don't shoot," he said, and raised his hands as if he were giving up, but as he raised them he drew the Colt. With a lightning blow to the temple, he erased Gliss's smirk. The second mate oozed onto his back.

From down the passage came a hail. "Did you get him, Gliss? What is happening?"

Fargo was out of the cabin before First Mate Berm was done shouting. He raced to the companionway and had a foot on the lowest step when it was filled by sailors pouring down from above. He whirled to run the other way but more were coming down the passage. They had him boxed in.

"No shooting!" Captain Strang bellowed from somewhere astern. "I want the bastard alive!"

So that was how it was. Fargo waded into the group blocking the steps. Clubbing heads wildly, he fought to reach the deck. Hands tore at arms. Fists glanced off his ribs and his shoulders. The fury of his attack took them off guard. A half dozen were crumpled heaps, bleeding and groaning, when he burst out onto the main deck. He needed to reach the rail and make it over the side but the deck swarmed with more sailors. He swung right; he swung left. They parted before his onslaught, enough for him to cross halfway to the bulwark. He thought he was going to make it, thought he would reach the side and dive over into the water and escape. Too late, it occurred to him that they were not fighting as fiercely as he was. They gave way much too easily. Almost as if they had been told to. Almost as if they were trying to delay him. *Why?* he wondered.

The answer came in the guise of a sharp command from Captain Strang. "Away from him, lads! Give them room!"

Just like that, the sailors scurried out of reach. Many were grinning.

"Now!" Captain Strang thundered.

From above Fargo's head came a new sound, an odd rustling that was not the rustling of the canvas but something else. Glancing up, he felt a fleeting instant of genuine fear. He had blundered, and blundered badly. Even as he attempted to leap clear, a large net enveloped him, a fishing net so heavy it crushed him flat. Instinctively, he thrust his arms out and they were instantly entangled. He sought to rise but the net closed around his legs. In two steps he was wrapped in a cocoon. He tottered, could not sustain his balance, and fell on his side.

Laughter greeted his downfall.

Even though it was useless, Fargo struggled to break free. All he succeeded in doing was tightening the net. He could barely move an arm or leg, and lay sucking breath into his lungs, nearly exhausted.

The ring of sailors closed. Through them shouldered

the walrus shape of Captain Theodore Strang. Hands on his hips, he looked down at Fargo and smirked in triumph. "To be honest, I didn't think it would be this easy."

"Go to hell."

Strang chuckled. "Now, now. You brought this on yourself by not leaving well enough alone. I explained how things are but you just wouldn't listen."

"Is Kean even on board?" Fargo asked.

"Where else would she be?" Strang rejoined. "I don't let her out of my sight except when work calls. She is in my cabin, chained by her ankle so she won't entertain foolish notions of sneaking off again."

"What now? Drop me over the side and drown me? Or have one of your boys slit my throat?"

Strang squatted and parted the strands, exposing Fargo's face. "In God's name, what do you take me for? I have a reputation for being tough, yes. But I am— what is that word you are so fond of? Ah, yes." He smiled a vicious smile. "I am fair. Ask anyone. In all my dealings I am always fair. I have never been accused of swindling or cheating or punishing more than is necessary. In your case that last is particularly relevant."

"What are you talking about?"

"All in good time," Strang replied. Crooking a finger at his first mate, he said, "You know what to do, Berm. I expect him for breakfast."

"Aye, aye, Captain."

Fargo had to endure the indignity of being carried below by six crewmen. The rest trailed after. To them he was a great amusement. They joked about how easily they had taken him captive, and dropped dark hints that he would not like what lay in store. Fargo said nothing.

Except for the three mates, who had cubbyholes all their own, the crew did not have the luxury of private quarters. They slept on the steerage floor, or secluded themselves in out-of-the-way nooks, where they were less likely to be disturbed.

Fargo was dumped on the steerage floor and surrounded. Daggers and knives were flourished. Berm and Gliss appeared holding rifles, which they trained on him.

"This is how we will it do, landlubber," the first mate said. "We are going to unravel the net. When I tell you, drop your pistol. If you don't, Mr. Gliss and I will blow holes in your head the size of walnuts. Don't think we won't. We are not virgins at spilling blood."

That brought a few guffaws.

"Begin," Berm directed the seaman.

For Fargo to resist would be suicide. He lay still, moving an arm or leg only when they told him to. He let go of the Colt when directed, and Gliss promptly snatched it up. At length the net was off and Fargo was on his belly and awaiting word to stand. To say he was mad was an understatement. He would gladly shoot them all down if he could, and hang the consequences.

"On your feet," First Mate Berm ordered.

Fargo slowly rose. His legs were stiff, his left arm sore where the net had twisted it.

"Take off your hat, your gun belt, and your boots."

Hesitating was only natural, but it earned Fargo a brutal jab to the base of his spine, courtesy of Gliss's rifle. The pain was excruciating. It nearly brought him to his knees.

"Understand something," Berm said. "When I tell you to do this or that, or any of the mates, for that matter, you are to treat it as if it were the captain speaking. Refuse, give us any trouble, any trouble at all, and we will dole out misery to suit us. Is that clear?"

Fargo nodded.

"You will answer aye, aye, sir, or lose your teeth."

A rifle butt raised to bash his mouth convinced Fargo to give in. "Aye, aye, sir."

"There. That wasn't so hard, was it?" Berm mocked him. "Now off with the hat, gun belt, and boots."

Fargo started to sit but was stopped by a poke in the back.

"Do it standing," Gliss said.

"I'll remember this," Fargo vowed. He was unprepared for the blow that caught him in the kidney. Berm was the culprit. Fargo pitched to his knees, agony washing over him in waves. He felt fingers grip his hair, felt his head jerked back.

"Thanks for reminding me," Berm said. "You are not to speak unless spoken to. Give us sass and you will wish you hadn't."

Fargo glared.

Second Mate Gliss sighed. "This one is going to be no end of aggravation. I can feel it in my bones."

Berm gave Fargo's head a violent shake. "Only a fool makes a bad situation worse. But enough. We don't want to spoil the surprise. Come morning the captain will reveal your fate." He released Fargo and stepped back. "I only hope I am there to see the look on your face."

Gliss chortled. "That makes two of us. And while the captain has forbidden us to tell you what's in store, landlubber, I can say this." He paused. "Before we are done with you, you will rue the day you set foot on our ship."

"Will he ever," a sailor remarked, and they all laughed.

8

Stepping into Theodore Strang's cabin was like stepping into a different world.

A whaler was a working ship, not a passenger vessel. Typical of her kind, the *Poseidon* was Spartan in the extreme. Nowhere was there a trace of that human tendency to savor the finer things of life. The *Poseidon* was not bedecked in luxuries. She had no soft parts. She was hard and always ready for action, befitting a warrior of the seas whose aquatic adversaries were capable of dashing her to pieces.

The exception, the sole exception in all her length and breath, was the captain's cabin. No luxury was spared in its adorning. From the ivory-inlaid table where Strang dined and studied his charts, to the fine china off which he ate, to the plush chairs and the bronze lamps and the bed wide enough for three and covered with an expensive quilt, the cabin was the ship's sole indulgence in the trappings of elegance.

Fargo paused in the doorway to take it all in. He had never been on a whaler before, and he never would set foot on one again if he lived to make it off this one.

"Come in, come in," Captain Strang urged from the head of the table. "You are to be my guest for breakfast."

A rough shove by Berm gave extra impetus to Fargo's first step, and he nearly tripped.

"None of that, First Mate," Strang scolded. "In here, at least, we will be civil. You will have plenty of opportunity to repay him, believe me." Strang gestured at a chair. "Have a seat, frontiersman. Make yourself comfortable. I took the liberty of pouring you a glass of whiskey."

The only other person at the table was a portrait in despair. Keanuenueokalani did not look up as Fargo entered. Before he could touch his chair to pull it out, a boy of fourteen or so, dressed in a white jacket and trousers, appeared out of empty air and pulled the chair out for him. The boy had a round face with wide, friendly eyes, an eager smile, and thick black curls. His skin was a coppery hue.

"This is Tubock," Captain Strang introduced him. "My cabin boy and errand boy and ship's mascot. He is from a small island in the South Pacific, an island you won't find on any chart. His people are savages. Twice each year they sacrifice the most beautiful of their maidens to their pagan gods."

Berm, Fargo noticed, had gone out and shut the door. He was alone with Kean and Strang and the boy. It was tempting to make his bid for freedom then and there.

As if privy to Fargo's thoughts, Strang grinned and said, "Lest you get any ideas, I will not be easy to overpower. The first mate and four crewmen are outside, and all I need do is yell."

"Why did you have me brought here?" Fargo asked. "To gloat?"

"How petty you must think me," Strang said. "No, believe it or not, I brought you here to treat you to a last courtesy before your sentence begins."

"My what?"

"More on that after a while." Strang turned. "Where are your manners, my dear? Welcome our guest, if you would be so kind."

Kean slowly raised her head. She did not say anything. She did not have to.

"And just so you know," Strang addressed Fargo, "I still have not laid a hand on her. I won't, either, until she consents to be my wife. She already is, mind you, as far as the crew is concerned and I am concerned, but I prefer she accept the inevitable of her own free will."

"You are one miserable son of a bitch," Fargo said.

Strang, surprisingly, laughed. "Your insults are wasted. Her father gave her to me, so she is mine to do with as I see fit. That I treat her with respect puts the lie to your barb." He motioned. "You neglect your whiskey."

Fargo picked up the glass. For a few moments, he debated dashing it in Strang's face, but it would have been a shame to waste the only whiskey he might have for a spell. He downed it in two gulps, smacked down the glass, and said, "Fill her again, bartender."

Strang seemed genuinely pleased. "You are a pleasure to deal with, sir. You ooze defiance, unlike the passive sheep who scamper to do my every bidding."

"Who are you kidding?" Fargo responded. "You like lording it over everyone."

"There you go again with the pettiness. But that, too, is untrue. Yes, on a ship like this, discipline is essential. The alternative is anarchy, and we can't have that." Strang raised a glass of wine and took a long sip. "Ah, ambrosia. I look forward to enjoying a lot more of the fruit of the vine when I am forced out to pasture, as I soon will be."

"You've lost me," Fargo admitted.

"Don't you keep up with current events?" Strang responded. "The industry I love—the glorious profession I have pursued my whole life long—will soon wither and fade. Whaling, Mr. Fargo, will be no more."

"How can that be?" Despite himself, Fargo was curious. The whaling trade had been around for as long as he could remember.

"Progress, Mr. Fargo. Just as beaver hats were once replaced by silk hats and the trapping industry died, so, too, with whaling. Why do we hunt whales, after all? Chiefly for their oil. Whale oil has brought light to the darkness, and did to candles what a new product is about to do to whale oil."

"New product?"

"You really must keep up with the times," Strang said. "Yes, Mr. Fargo. A new type of oil. Petroleum, they call it. It is far cheaper than whale oil and a lot easier to come by. I hate the very word. It means an end to all I am." He glowered, but not at Fargo. "Oh, I imagine there will still be some slight demand for whale oil, and the killing of whales will go on, but not on the scale to which we are accustomed. No, this new petroleum has turned out to be the whale's best friend."

Fargo could almost sympathize. A day was coming, and not far off, when there would no longer be a need for men like him, for scouts and trailblazers. Eventually the westward tide would push past the Mississippi River to the Pacific Ocean. Towns and cities would dot the prairies and the mountains, bringing an end to the frontier.

Strang was speaking. "But I did not invite you here to discuss business. Let's fill our bellies, and then we can get to the matter at hand." He clapped his hands.

Tubock brought in the food: silver trays heaped high with scrambled eggs, with bacon, with toast, with flap-jacks, with fruit. Piping hot coffee was provided, as well as a silver bowl filled with sugar and another with cream.

Fargo did not hold back. He ate fit to burst. He had a hunch this was his last good meal, if Strang had any-thing to say about it. So he had two helpings of nearly everything and washed the food down with five cups of coffee. When he finally pushed his plate back, Strang regarded him with amusement.

"It is a wonder you aren't a whale yourself, with the appetite you have. Even Gliss would be hard put to hold his own, and I have never met anyone who likes food as much as he does."

Fargo folded his hands and waited. Now that the meal was almost over, the other shoe was about to drop.

Strang wagged a finger at the table and the trappings. "You will admit, I trust, that was damned decent of me. A treat for the condemned, as it were."

"I must have missed the part where I stood trial," Fargo said.

"Poke fun if you want. But that is exactly what has occurred. Oh, not by any court of law. You have been tried by me and judged by me according to your crimes. Now I am about to pronounce sentence."

"I've said it before and I will say it again," Fargo replied. "You are a miserable son of a bitch."

Strang rested his elbows on the table and made a tepee of his fingers. "Surely you are aware a ship's captain has certain prerogatives? I am lord and master here. My word is law. My decisions have the weight of true authority. I am often compelled to judge men for breaches of discipline. Just as I have judged you for your crimes."

"Crimes?" Fargo said.

"You do remember pushing one of my men over a railing? And you do recall shooting two others? Acts that would be considered criminal by any court in the land."

"I did all that in self-defense."

"Which is the only reason I don't have you hanged from the yardarm, as you suggested," Strang said with a smirk. "My men were a little too overenthusiastic. For that they paid. And now you must pay. I cannot permit what you have done to go unpunished or my crew will begin to doubt my fitness to command."

"That's as good an excuse as any, I suppose," Fargo said.

"Oh, it is much more than that, I assure you. A captain must rule with an iron hand. Otherwise his men start to think they can do as they please, and before you know it, the malcontents and layabouts have taken over and the captain must practically beg to get work done." Strang paused. "I do not beg."

"So let's hear this sentence of yours."

Strang sat back in his chair and adopted a serious expression. "I wouldn't be so glib, were I you. I do not do this lightly. It is only after careful consideration that I have decided to shanghai you."

"To what?"

"You are being shanghaied, Mr. Fargo, forced to work as a ship's hand."

Fargo had heard of the practice. Usually the culprits were captains too cheap to hire a full crew so they shanghaied a few men, invariably drunks who came out of their stupor miles out to sea and with no recourse but to do as they were told or be tossed overboard. This was the first time he ever heard of someone being shanghaied as punishment. He said as much.

Theodore Strang grinned. "A good captain adapts to circumstances as they arise. I should point out that I am being a lot easier on you than my crew wanted me to be. They were all for quartering you and feeding the remains to sharks, or keelhauling you from here to our next port of call. You really should thank me."

"Go to hell."

"There you go again. But I won't let you get to me." Strang snapped his fingers as if remembering something. "Oh. You might be interested to learn that the term of your involuntary indenture, if you will, is for three years."

Fargo nearly came out of his chair. "If you think I'm going to stand for this—"

Strang held up a hand. "I thought I had made it clear by now. You do not have a choice." Raising his voice, he yelled, "Mr. Berm, if you please."

The door opened and in came the first mate and four sailors. One of the sailors carried shackles. Berm stood to one side and trained a rifle on Fargo while the other four surrounded the chair.

"Be so kind as to stick out your legs," Captain Strang said.

Fargo was not about to meekly submit. He came up swinging but they were ready for him. Two grabbed his arms while a third tackled him about the waist, and almost before he could blink, he was flat on his back with the weight of all three on his limbs and chest. They showed no particular joy in what they were doing.

The fourth man came up. He knelt at Fargo's feet and clamped a metal ring to Fargo's leg just above the ankle. He went to clamp the other leg, and stiffened. "Ho. Cap-

62

tain, sir! Take a look at what he has here. A clever rascal, this."

Strang rose and came over. Berm, too, wanted to see.

The sailor had pulled Fargo's pant leg up, revealing his ankle sheath and the Arkansas toothpick. Drawing the knife, the man passed it to Strang.

"Clever, indeed, Wells. It's a good thing you found this or my life would not be worth a thimble of seawater. Someday when I least expected, he would have slit my throat. I commend you."

"Thank you, sir."

Fargo watched as Strang took the toothpick to a desk and placed it in the top drawer.

Wells finished with the shackles and stood back. The other three hauled Fargo to his feet. He looked down. Never, ever had he been as mad as he was at that moment. The shackles bit into his flesh, but not deep. Three feet of chain permitted him to move about, but he would not be doing any running or jumping.

"What? No threats? No bluster?" Captain Strang asked. "The usual line is that if it is the last thing you ever do, you will see me in Davy Jones's locker."

The sailors found that humorous.

"No?" Strang said. "Well, then. We have concluded our business. The condemned has had his last supper, my hearties, and can now be put to work doing whatever the mates see fit. But understand, Berm, he is not to be mistreated. No one is to beat him unless he deserves it. Don't deprive him of food or water without my permission. He is no use to us weak and broken."

"Aye, aye, sir."

"Any last comment?" Strang asked Fargo.

Fargo looked at Keanuenueokalani. Her sorrow had deepened and her eyes were moist.

"I am sorry, Skye. This is my fault. If I had not sought your help, you would not be in irons."

Strang's cruel mouth curled in an indulgent smile. "How very noble of you, my dear. But do not waste tears on your would-be knight. Any man who meddles where he is not wanted must expect to pay for his audacity." He nodded at Berm. "Take the landlubber away. Assign the third mate to watch over him until he learns what is expected. For the first week or so, he is to be lashed to the mainmast at night to give him a taste of what is in store if he misbehaves."

"You heard the captain," Berm said. "Up on deck with you."

Fargo shuffled to the door, the heavy chain rattling with every step. It would take some getting used to before he could move freely. Not that he intended to wear the leg irons that long. Then and there he silently vowed that before he was done, the captain and crew of the *Poseidon* were going to pay for what they had done to him.

They were going to pay in blood.

9

The next morning the *Poseidon* set sail.

The huge anchor was hoisted, the whaler hauled from the wharf, the sails unfurled, and like a bird spreading its wings and taking flight, the great ship spread its canvas and sailed out of the congested harbor toward the open ocean.

Captain Strang loomed on the quarterdeck barking orders, which the crew scurried to obey. They swarmed up the rigging like so many monkeys, with an agility born of long experience. Each man knew what was expected of him and knew he must do his job well or suffer the captain's wrath.

Fargo had spent the night tied to the mainmast. He was untied before the sun rose so no one on shore would notice and possibly report his captivity to the law.

The third mate, whose name was Collins, did both the tying and the untying. He was not happy about having to ride herd on Fargo, and he did not hide his resentment. "Why me?" he grumbled at one point. "Any of the crew could nursemaid you, but the captain picked me." He was a sallow, thin man prone to bad temper. He was not as prone to bathing, much to the regret of anyone who had to stand close to him.

An incident of note occurred before they set sail. Collins came up from below and over to the mainmast, yawning and scratching himself. He stared hard at Fargo, then said, "The captain wants you let loose before it gets light. Don't try anything or you will regret it."

Fargo was tired of the threats. But he had something more important on his mind. "I need to talk to him."

"To Captain Strang? What for?"

"I'll tell him in person. Go let him know."

Collins uttered a brittle laugh; then, without warning, he kicked Fargo in the shin. "Get something straight, mister. I tell you what to do. You do not tell me. And no, I won't fetch the captain. He doesn't like to be disturbed without good cause."

Fargo fought down the pain and did not let his anger get the better of him. "It's important. I am asking you, man to man."

"The answer is still no."

"Do this for me and I will do something for you," Fargo said.

Again the brittle laugh. "What can you possibly do for me that will make it worth my while?"

"I won't kill you."

Collins gave a start and took a step back. "What's this? There will be none of that kind of talk or I will have you whipped. The captain wants you alive, but there is nothing to stop me from having the skin flayed from your back."

"And there is nothing to stop me from taking a bucket or a hammer and caving in your skull someday when you won't be expecting it."

Collins clenched his fists. "I don't scare easy."

"Hear me out," Fargo said. "I don't like this any better than you do. I could give you a lot of trouble. I could refuse to do any work. Whip me all you want. You'll find I still won't cooperate. Strang won't like that. He won't like it one bit that you can't control one man. Maybe he'll think you don't deserve to be third mate and give the job to someone else."

"You bastard," Collins said.

"I'm not done. The other side of the coin is for me to not give you trouble. For me to do whatever you want me to do without giving you sass. It will make things easy for both of us, and it will please Strang and keep you in his good graces." Fargo paused. "Do me this one

66

favor, Collins. Let me talk to him and I give you my word I won't make your life hell."

The third mate's ferret face wrinkled in thought. "You have your nerve—I'll say that. But you also make a good point. The captain does not suffer incompetents. And I like being third mate. It's a step to second mate, or even first, and that's as high as I can expect to rise in this world." He chewed on his lower lip, then nodded. "Very well. I will take you at your word. I will go tell the captain you want to see him. But mark me, landlubber, and mark me well. If you have deceived me, if you break your promise and give me grief, it could be you will suffer an accident one day when you least expect. With those chains on your legs, you can't swim very well. Think what would happen if you were to fall over the side."

"I will keep my word so long as we are at sea," Fargo promised.

Collins stood there a moment longer. "Very well. I just pray the captain is in good spirits. When he is in one of his moods, he will bite a man's head off as soon as look at him."

Fargo waited in a state of anxious dread. It took forever before a large bulk filled the companionway and came across the deck with the third mate in tow.

"This does not bode well," Theodore Strang said. "Explain to me why you have imposed on my time and good graces."

"It's about my horse."

Strang cocked his head. "Just when a man thinks he has heard everything. You are being shanghaied and all you are worried about is some dumb animal?"

"My Ovaro. He is at a stable on Montgomery Street. I'm only paid up until the end of the week. If I don't claim him, the stable owner can sell him or do whatever he wants."

"So?" Strang said. "Why is that any concern of mine?"

"I have a room at a boardinghouse on Fremont. My poke is wrapped in my bedroll. There is enough money to board my horse for six months, and extra besides. Send someone to fetch it and pay the stableman and you can keep whatever is left over."

"How generous of you," Strang said.

Collins started past him, snarling, "Of all the nerve! You made it sound important enough for me to bother the captain. I should bloody you good." But a thick arm across his chest stopped him.

"Simmer down, Third Mate," Strang rumbled. "It's good that he brought this up."

"It is, sir?"

"He might have friends who will wonder where he got to and snoop around asking questions. Maybe he has mentioned the *Poseidon* or myself to them."

"We will be long gone before anyone comes looking."

"True. But I would rather not be connected to his disappearance. Remember Captain Rogers? He shanghaied a man, and the man's brother got wind of it, and the next time Rogers was in port, the brother shot him." Strang clasped his big hands behind his broad back. "Better for us to cover our tracks, I think. Go find Wells. Send him to the boardinghouse. Have him gather up all of Fargo's effects and bring them on board. Instruct him to stop at the stable first and pay to have the horse boarded for six months."

"As you wish, sir," Collins said, his tone implying he considered it a waste of money.

"Have Wells tells the stable owner that Fargo here has decided to go on a sea voyage."

"To where, sir?"

"Eh? Oh, make it Alaska. That way if anyone ever does come looking for him, they will look in the wrong place." As the third mate scampered off, Strang turned to Fargo. "Satisfied?"

"I'm in your debt. It won't stop me from doing what I have to when the time comes, but for this I will make it quick and painless."

"The audacity," Strang said, but not with rancor. "You puzzle me. This horse means that much to you?"

Fargo tried to shrug but couldn't, lashed as he was to the mast. "No more or less than this ship means to you."

"Ah. Now that I can understand." Strang gazed about them. "The *Poseidon* is everything to me, frontiersman. Mother, father, bosom friend. If our treasure is where our heart is, as someone once put it, then this ship is both my treasure and my heart. My very life, if you will." He breathed deep and let out a long breath. "I would rather die than see her come to harm. I respect your attachment to your horse." He turned and went below.

Fargo had sagged against the mast. At least he had one less worry.

Then came the dawn, and the mad scramble to set sail. An orderly scramble for all that, with each doing his duty and no slack. At length the freshly barnacle-free bow of the *Poseidon* was out of the bay and plying the waves of the vast ocean.

On most ships, Fargo later learned, it was the pilot who steered the vessel from anchorage to open water, but Captain Strang always took the *Poseidon* out himself. He was not one of those captains who stayed in the comfort of their cabins and let those under them do all the work. Strang did as much work as any man under him. More, even, since he performed duties the mates could just as well do. They took it as a matter of course.

Once out to sea, the crew settled into a routine. There was always something to do. Rigging to replace, canvas to mend, harpoons to be sharpened, the whole ship to be swept and wiped down and always kept clean. Captain Strang did not tolerate sloppiness. If he found a rope left lying underfoot, the culprit was apt to find himself going without food for two or three days to teach him his error.

Strang never beat his men, never had them whipped, as some captains did. He did not need to. They feared his anger, and quaked at the thought of punishment. Fargo overheard several allow as how Strang was stern, yes, but he was also just. Strang never punished anyone without cause, and the punishment always fit the misdeed. To a man, the crew held Strang in sincere respect.

Fargo learned something else of value. The fifth day out, he heard the cook tell a new crew member about the time another captain took exception to a comment Strang made about the captain's ability and went at Strang with his fists flying.

"It was a sight to see, lad," the cook related with awe in his tone. "Captain Strang took the best that other captain could dish out, and nary batted an eye. One punch Strang threw, just one punch, and that other captain was on his back with his jaw broke and bits of broken teeth dribbling over his lip. I saw it with my own eyes, and I am here to vow, Captain Strang is as strong as Samson, and that's no lie."

That walrus body, it turned out, was compact muscle.

Third Mate Collins never lacked for things for Fargo to do. Fargo swept. He wiped. He polished. He emptied buckets. He helped the cook. He helped the carpenter.

The rest of the crew ignored him except for occasional glares. They would not even talk to him. Fargo asked Collins about that one evening as they stood on the bow waiting for the call to go below and eat.

The third mate snickered. "The short of it is, they hate your guts. You shot three of our own, if you'll recall, and sailors are not a forgiving lot when it comes to harm to them and their friends. Were it up to them, they would as soon dump you over the side and be done with you."

"It doesn't matter that the three I shot were about to shoot me?"

"Not a whit," Collins said. "All that counts, so far as you are concerned, is that the captain has decreed you are not to be harmed. That is the only reason you still breathe."

Twice each day Keanuenueokalani was permitted to come up on deck and take a stroll, always in Strang's company, so approaching her was out of the question. Several times Fargo caught her staring at him when Strang was not looking. She gave the impression she wanted to talk to him as much as he wanted to talk to her.

The eighth day out, Fargo was mopping the forecastle deck, or the fo'c'sle, as the sailors pronounced it, when a shadow fell across him and Collins, who was next to him at the time. The third mate jumped and turned, blurting, "Captain Strang! I didn't hear you come up, sir."

"I wanted a word with our shanghai and you both." Strang moved to the rail. He had his arms behind him, as he often did, and moved with a lightness an Apache would admire.

"Sir?" Collins said.

"Starting tonight, he will sleep with the rest of the crew below. Each evening he will be permitted an hour to himself. You need no longer watch him every minute of the day." Strang chuckled. "It is not as if he is going anywhere."

"Aye, aye, Captain."

Fargo stopped sweeping and leaned on the broom.

"What do you think of our watery world, frontiersman? It is a far cry from the world you are accustomed to, is it not?"

"A sea of water, a sea of grass," Fargo said. "In my world there are buffalo and deer and prairie dogs. In yours there are fish and sharks and whales. It's not all that different."

"Really? I would have thought you would think otherwise. But I should extend a compliment. You have taken to my world much more readily than I would take to yours. Collins tells me that not once since we set sail have you been seasick."

"I spend a lot of time in the saddle."

"Interesting. You imply the motion of your horse has made you immune to the motion of my ship? I had not considered that." Strang faced them. "It is unfortunate we had to meet under these circumstances, Mr. Fargo. I find myself liking you."

Fargo did not share the feeling so he did not reply.

71

"Keep behaving yourself and eventually those leg irons might come off," Strang informed him. "It might surprise you to learn that I cannot stand to see a man in chains. Maybe it is my love of the open sea and freedom."

"But you are not losing any sleep over me being in leg irons," Fargo said.

Captain Strang frowned. "Again you bait me. I suppose I have it coming but it is tiresome. With the exception of Keanuenueokalani, I might well be the only friend you have on this vessel."

"If you are a friend, I don't need enemies."

"I can see it is pointless to try and get on your good side," Strang remarked. Tsk-tsking to himself, he strolled forward.

Collins whistled softly. "You have backbone, mister, but you sure are dumb."

"Think so, do you?"

"I know so. Make the captain mad enough and he might change his mind about keeping you alive. Or is it that you *want* to be fed to the sharks?"

10

"A spout! Avast! By God, it's a spout!"

The *Poseidon* was two weeks out of San Francisco. Fargo was helping the cook. He had been told to slice potatoes and had just started when the cry rang out above them.

The cook, in the act of chopping onions, jumped to his feet. "Did you hear?" he excitedly asked. "Did you hear the lookout?"

Again a cry rang out. "Thar she blows, boys! Three of them! Oh, hurry, boys, hurry, or we will lose the beasts!"

Throwing down his knife and the onion, the cook swiped at his apron and dashed for the passage. "Come on! Don't dawdle! We don't want to miss this."

Fargo hurried as best he was able wearing the leg irons. He had learned to take short, gliding steps. That way the chain was less likely to snag and trip him. From all over the ship came shouts and the stamp of feet as everyone on board rushed topside. He could guess what the ruckus was about, but that did not prepare him for the bedlam that had burst over the whaler like a storm-tossed wave.

"There's a hump!" a sailor yelled, pointing.

"And there go flukes under!" cried another.

"To windward they go! To windward!"

Loudest of all was the captain's bellow. "Man the boats, damn your bones! Time to earn your keep, children!"

Most of the activity swirled around three boats being

readied for lowering. Each needed rowers, a man to handle the rudder, and the harpooner. Fargo, curious to witness the unfolding chase, had moved near to one of the boats when a heavy hand fell on his shoulder.

"What think you, frontiersman?" Captain Strang asked. His eyes gleamed with the thrill of the hunt. "Are you up for it?"

Fargo did not know what he meant.

"Care to try your hand at my world?" Captain Strang propelled him to the boat, saying, "Make way! Make room for a passenger!"

The looks Fargo was given showed what the men in the boat thought of the proposition, but no one dared complain. Fargo was given no time to object or argue. He was bodily lifted and dumped in between the last seat and the rudder. Then Captain Strang climbed in and moved to the bow.

Fargo had been told that captains rarely went after whales. Few were able harpooners. Strang, his crew had proudly boasted, was a notable exception. He would not have his men do anything he would not do himself, and that included slaying their leviathan quarry. Watching Strang heft a harpoon, Fargo had little doubt he was as good as they claimed. Whatever Strang did, he did well. Begrudgingly, Fargo felt more than a twinge of respect.

With admirable swiftness the boats were soon in the water and the rowers were bending their backs to the oars. Like falcons unleashed and loosed on prey, the three boats flew after the whales.

It had all happened so fast that Fargo had little time to collect his wits. Now that he did, he realized he was in chains in a small boat on a windswept ocean in pursuit of three of the largest creatures in all creation. It occurred to him that if the boat went down, so would he. He could hardly swim with his legs fettered.

A shout from Gliss, who had the tiller, brought him out of himself. "Two humps, Captain! No! Three!"

Fargo saw them then, clearly, and for one of the few times in his life, he was struck with absolute wonder. The creatures were huge, gigantic beyond anything he had imagined. He always thought grizzlies were giants, but compared to a whale, a grizzly was a minnow. His mind balked at their immensity. The whales were over sixty feet long, ton upon ton of massive might, yet incredibly graceful in motion. The arc of their huge bodies and the perpetual hiss of their passage were breathtaking.

"Faster, you grog swillers!" Captain Strang thundered. "Put your backs to those oars, by God!"

Wells happened to be manning an oar near Fargo, and he said as he stroked, "Those are sperm whales, landlubber. Next to right whales, they are the whales we most love to catch." He strained and grunted. "Those three are males. A bachelor school, we call it. It's the big one we want. He'll render the most oil."

Fargo could see that one of the whales was in fact considerably larger than the other two. It was also the fastest, and ahead of the others. But the three boats were rapidly narrowing the gap.

"Row and pull!" Captain Strang thundered. "Row and pull, my hearties! We close! Do you see the white water? We close!"

Fargo saw that where the sperm whales cleaved the surface, the water was flung in white, hissing spray, and when they submerged, the water became a white, hissing froth. Always that hissing, that never-ending hissing.

The other two boats were making for the smaller whales. But not Strang. He was after the large one. He stood in the bow, harpoon in hand, the line in coils, his whole muscular frame aquiver with the heat of his passion. "Keep pulling! Keep pulling! We almost have him!"

Wells glanced at Fargo. "We don't often see sperms in these waters. But we never pass up a prospect."

His gaze glued to Strang and the whale, Fargo absently asked, "How many do you kill on a voyage like this?"

"Our last time out, over eight hundred."

Fargo blinked, his concentration shattered. "How many?"

"You heard aright. Eight hundred and twelve, I think it was. Enough for almost three thousand barrels of whale oil. My shares were the best ever."

Whalers, Fargo had learned, were not paid a salary or paid by the day, but by the number of shares they were allotted. Each share was worth a percentage of the profits. A captain might have four or five hundred shares, or half the profits. The first mate, typically, received two hundred shares, the second mate one hundred, and so on, down to the crew, who usually received three shares apiece. That could amount to upward of two thousand dollars in a day and age when most men earned barely four hundred dollars a year.

Fargo leaned forward. He did not want to miss what happened next. They were almost close enough. The sperm whale was a moving ebony mountain, the skin ridged and pitted, not smooth as he had thought it might be. The hump of the dorsal fin reminded him of the hump of a buffalo. Behind it was a bony sawtooth clear to the tail. The pectoral fins seemed small for the whale's size. The flukes, on the other hand, were enormous. They struck the surface with crashing impact.

Captain Strang raised his harpoon. He was focused on the whale and only on the whale. His walrus body did not appear ungainly now; it was poised for the purpose for which the man lived, every sinew cast in steel.

In the excitement of the moment, Gliss suddenly shouted, "Now, Captain, now! Oh, sweet God, we will lose him!"

Fargo rose higher. He picked the perfect instant. For just then Captain Strang let fly, the line trailing after. The harpoon buried itself in the whale, and in a twinkling the line was taut and the boat leaped ahead. It skipped the surface like a thrown flat stone, smacking down hard enough to jar Fargo to the bone. A wet mist shrouded them.

Quickly, Strang readied another harpoon. They drew in near, and Strang cast again. His aim was unerring. No Comanche ever threw a lance more accurately. The harpoon pierced where it should.

76

"Beware the tail!" Strang bellowed. "Watch how she rolls!"

The great whale was in its death throes. Its giant jaws opened and closed as it rolled. From the blowhole came a strange clacking sound. For all its gargantuan dimensions, for all its immense size, the creature had been brought low by a toothpick of iron and wood.

Fargo saw the water around the whale become red with blood. So much blood, it astonished him. Suddenly the whale's huge head shot up and from the blowhole came another spout, only this one was bright crimson. Blood rain fell on the boat, spattering Fargo from head to toe.

"The beast won't die!" Captain Strang exclaimed, and prepared to throw another harpoon.

But as abruptly as the whale had righted itself, it now rolled onto its side and was still. The blowhole stopped quivering, and the fins stopped their feeble movement.

"At last!" a sailor said.

"I've seen many last longer," commented another.

"The captain always casts true," mentioned a third. "He hasn't ever lost a boat."

Captain Strang heard every word. "No, I have not, and I do not intend to start. A man must be good at something, by God."

At that, a sailor chuckled. "And you are one of the best, Captain, unless you have taken to covering yourself with red paint."

Fargo was transfixed by the whale. Even dead it was a marvel. He had a childish impulse to reach out and touch it, but the rattle of his chain when he moved a leg deterred him.

The clink drew Strang's attention. "Well, frontiersman? What say you? Is there the like anywhere on your prairies or high amid your mountains? Will you concede this is the grandest hunt of all?"

"I'll never forget it," was the most Fargo would admit.

"Bah," said Strang. "You are parsimonious with your praise because you are jealous of our strife. There is no comparison with your puny buffalo."

That brought laughter.

"Now, now, boys," Captain Strang said. "I intended no insult. To each man, his particular vanities. All I am saying is that the slaying of a hairy brute no bigger than a horse pales when compared to the slaying of our colossus of the seas."

"That it does, Captain," Gliss declared loudly. "That it does."

Strang's gaze fixed on him. "Thank you for reminding me. What was that you shouted right before I cast the first harpoon? Were you trying to jinx my arm?"

Gliss shriveled at the rebuke. "As heaven is my witness, Captain, not then, not ever."

"See that you keep a watch on that tongue of yours, Second Mate," Strang cautioned. "A harpooner at the moment of harpooning is as close to the Almighty as this life gets."

Lines were secured and the rowers bent to the arduous task of making to meet the *Poseidon*. Fargo was surprised to note how far they had traveled. The chase had taken them more than a half mile from the ship. To the south, one of the other boats had also made a kill, but the third boat had missed and was already well toward the *Poseidon*.

Gliss uttered a bark of amusement and exclaimed, "Here comes the first of the toothsome vultures, lads. It never takes them long, does it?"

Fargo looked, and his skin crawled.

Slicing through the sea toward them was a high tapering fin. A slight hiss could be heard as it drew close to their catch. Just when he thought it would collide with the whale, the fin sank with barely a ripple. A furious agitation roiled the water, and shortly a new patch of blood turned to black.

"Old man shark has helped himself to a nibble," a sailor said.

"There will be plenty more before our carving is done," Wells declared.

Fargo saw another fin approaching. "You don't mind?"

Wells snorted. "We might as well mind the moon or

the stars. Sharks live to eat. Who does the killing is of no matter to their mouths. Some days we have hundreds come to feast. They churn the sea in their frenzy, and woe to the man who slips and falls in."

"But you lose some of your catch," Fargo said.

"A thousand sharks could show and no more than scratch the meat pie," Wells answered.

Fargo thought of how buzzards and coyotes and other scavengers could reduce a buffalo carcass to gleaming white bones in only a few hours.

Since the other whale was nearer, the *Poseidon* went to her first. Block and tackle were brought out and the whale lashed to her side. Then, sluggish as if fat with blubber, the *Poseidon* made for her other offspring. By then Strang's boatmen had brought his catch to within a few hundred yards. It, too, was floated and secured.

There was no celebration. For the whalers this was work, and work they did, butchery on a scale that mentally staggered Fargo. It was as if ten thousand elk were being carved up at once.

The carving wasn't random. Just as Indians never let any part of a buffalo go to waste, so, too, did whalers have a use for almost all of their quarry. The blubber would be turned into oil. From the gut came ambergris, which smelled vile in the extreme. But when the ambergris was exposed to air, a remarkable change took place. The ambergris became as fragrant as a flower.

The first step was for the crew to separate the head from the body. The head was then hung from a cable. A huge hook was stuck into the body and half a dozen crewmen put their backs to the windlass. Bit by bit the blubber was peeled away, much as an orange peel was peeled from an orange. What was left of the body was cut loose, after a few choice parts were saved for eating.

Then the head was raised higher. The brains were removed. Two men clambered on top and a bucket was lowered to scoop out the waxy, and extremely valuable, spermaceti.

Fargo was a fascinated observer. For a while he almost forgot he was there against his will. He was reminded when he went to move to a better vantage point and his leg irons clanked. Another reminder came with a whiff of perfume and a whisper only his ears heard.

"We need to talk." Keanuenueokalani was at his elbow, standing so she was not visible to Strang, who was overseeing the butchery. Like Fargo, she wore leg irons.

For a few moments Fargo was speechless with surprise.

"Didn't you hear me? We need to talk."

"I heard," Fargo said.

"I have an idea how we can free ourselves of our shackles and be rid of Theodore Strang. Are you interested?"

"Need you ask?"

"It is dangerous," Kean said. "It might well get both of us killed."

"Just so I take Strang with me," Fargo said. "What do you have in mind?"

11

It was the next day, as Fargo was cleaning whale blood from the deck, that he sensed someone behind him and turned. Out of instinct he started to drop his right hand to the hip where his Colt should be. "You don't have better things to do than sneak up on people?"

Captain Strang had his hands behind his back and wore a thoughtful expression. "I have always been light on my feet," he commented. His gaze was on the sea. "To be honest, I hardly realized you were there."

Fargo was working unguarded. Collins no longer watched over him every minute of the day. It wasn't as if he would try to escape in the middle of the ocean. He bent to his mop but stopped when Strang had more to say.

"Do you appreciate the finer ironies of life, Fargo? I do. And it is ironic that you went to so much trouble and are now in irons for nothing."

Fargo realized Kean had put her plan into effect but he must feign ignorance. "What are you talking about?"

"Keanuenueokalani—the lovely maiden you tried to wrest from my grasp. She has admitted that I am not the ogre she painted me as, and she is willing to become my wife."

"No," Fargo said, trying to make it sound as if he was shocked.

"Yes. All that effort you went to, wasted." Strang smiled serenely. "My fondest wish has come true. I have wanted that girl for so long, and in about two weeks I will have her."

"Two weeks?" Fargo repeated.

"That is about how long it will take us to reach Hawaii," Strang said. "You see, she set a condition. She will marry me only if we have the traditional ceremony of her people." He paused. "I did not intend to put in at Hawaii. My plan was to strike off for the South Seas and spend a year whaling. But the delay will be worth it if it means she finally becomes mine."

Fargo hid his relief. "I'm happy for you," he said, with just enough spite for Strang to notice.

The captain laughed. "You are a good hater. I admire that, because I, too, am not one to forgive and forget. Maybe I will let you come ashore and witness the ceremony. Under guard, of course, and with a gun at your back so you won't do anything foolish."

"The Hawaiian government won't mind you forcing her to marry you?"

Strang's good humor evaporated. "You haven't been paying attention. Keanuenueokalani has decided of her own free will to take the vow. As for the government, why would the king and the council of chiefs object? Their subjects are free to marry foreigners if they want."

"Lucky for you," Fargo remarked.

The captain did not seem to hear him. "Besides, Hawaii depends on the whaling trade for much of its income. They would not do anything to make the whalers mad."

"After you marry her? What then?"

"Eh?" Strang glanced sharply at him. "How do you mean?"

"Are you going to drag her all over the Pacific with you? Or leave her in Hawaii until you get back?" Fargo knew it was considered a bad omen to have a woman on board. He had heard a few of the crew muttering about it, but they were careful to mutter when Strang was nowhere around.

"Need you ask? After waiting so long to have her, do you honestly think I will leave her behind?"

Fargo went back to mopping the blood. He was aware that Strang was still there but he ignored him.

"I must say, you surprise me."

"Is that so?" Fargo imagined breaking the mop handle in half and spearing an end into Strang's chest.

"You have been remarkably well behaved since you were shanghaied. Most men in your shoes would rant and rave and throw fits a good long while before they accepted the inevitable."

Fargo shrugged. "I like to gamble, and a good gambler knows when to buck the odds and when not to."

"In other words, you are biding your time until you think the time is right," Strang said. "Your self-control is exceptional."

"I like breathing," Fargo said.

"Ah. Self-preservation. I have a strong streak of that myself. It is why I will never give you the chance you seek. Give up any hope you have of besting me. You will only be disappointed."

"You talk a good fight."

"I am good with more than words," Strang said.

"So you say," Fargo responded, "but I noticed you let your men do your fighting for you."

"I see," Strang said, and walked off.

Fargo figured that was the last he would see of the lord of the *Poseidon* for a while, but he was mistaken. He was almost done mopping when feet scuffed the deck and he raised his head to find sailors gathering from fore and aft. Berm, Gliss, and Collins were among them.

The first mate came up to him and smirked. "You have stepped in it now, landlubber."

Gliss nodded. "I would not care to be you for all the gold there ever was."

"I'm looking forward to it," Collins said. "Not that I have anything against you personally, plainsman. But we can do with a little entertainment."

"Don't worry about broken bones and the like," Berm said. "We don't have a doctor on board, but Gliss here can mend just about anything this side of a gut wound."

"Those are the worst," the second mate agreed. "It's impossible to stop infection from setting in."

Fargo did not ask them what they were talking about. He had guessed. He leaned on the mop handle.

As the Red Sea parted for Moses, the crew parted for their master. Theodore Strang had stripped off his coat, shirt, and hat, and was naked from the waist up. His bulky body was a granite block, his arms thick clubs. He put his big hands on his hips and bobbed his chin at the first mate. "Undo his leg irons, Berm. This will be as fair as I can make it."

"Aye, aye, sir."

The first mate tossed the mop to Collins. Berm produced a key, squatted, and removed first the left shackle and then the right. Tossing the irons to Gliss, he stepped back.

The sailors had formed a ring. Excited murmuring rippled among them, but stopped when Captain Strang motioned for quiet.

"Some of you are wondering what this is about. I will tell you." Strang bobbed his chin at Fargo. "Our shanghai thinks I like to let others do my fighting for me. All of you know that is not the case. I have said many times, and I will say it again now: I harpoon my own whales. I intend to show him he is mistaken."

"What if I don't want to fight you?" Fargo asked.

"Then it is your courage that will be called into question," Strang said. "Frankly, were I you, I would bow out anyway. You don't stand a prayer. I have been challenged many times but I have never lost."

"What is that old saying?" Fargo countered. "There is a first time for everything." But he did not feel nearly as confident as he tried to sound. Strang outweighed him by a good fifty to sixty pounds, and he had no doubt the man was every whit as formidable as he claimed.

"Do you mind if we wager on the outcome, sir?" Berm asked.

"Not at all," Strang said.

The first mate held coins aloft. "I have ten dollars on the captain. Who is willing to place ten on buckskin?"

There were no takers.

Captain Strang laced his thick fingers together and cracked his knuckles. "It appears there is a distinct lack of confidence in you," he told Fargo. "But don't feel bad. The men have seen me whip others. They know what I can do."

Fargo lifted each leg a few times. They felt strangely light, the result, he reckoned, of wearing leg irons for so long. Other than where his ankles were chafed, neither leg bothered him.

"I will permit you to bow out if such is your wish," Captain Strang offered. "There isn't a man here who would not do the same. No one will think less of you."

"Except me." Not that Fargo cared what the sailors thought of him.

"You will regret your decision," Strang said. "But I will go easy on you." He flexed his legs and windmilled his arms, turning in a circle as he did. Midway, he abruptly stopped and focused on the quarterdeck.

Fargo had already spotted her.

Keanuenueokalani stood at the rail. She met Strang's curious stare with a smile. She still wore legs irons. Despite them, she stood straight and proud, her beauty undiminished.

Strang cleared his throat. "What are you doing there, my dear? I thought I made it plain that I prefer you stay below."

"You did say, my husband to be," Kean replied, "that I could come up for fresh air and exercise now and again, did you not?"

"Yes, I did," Strang conceded, "but now is not the time. Mr. Fargo and I are about engage in a bit of ugliness."

"So I heard," Kean said. "If you think you must, then by all means, go ahead. But I cannot help but think that for grown men to behave this way is more than a little childish."

"You don't understand, my dear," Strang told her. "He has insulted me. I must prove myself, not only to him, but to my men and my own self."

"You are Theodore Strang," Kean said. "You have nothing to prove to anyone, least of all the dogs who serve under you."

"Now, now," Strang said. "They are my crew, and I will not have them abused. They have treated you with high regard, have they not? They do not even swear in your presence."

"The only reason they behave is because they are afraid of you," Kean said. "Fear keeps them in line, not special respect for me."

"You do not give them enough credit," Strang objected.

Or it could be, Fargo reflected, that the captain gave them too much. He had seen the looks they gave her when Strang was not around. Raw lust was as rampant as lice.

"Are you refusing me permission to stay on deck?" Kean asked.

"Don't put words in my mouth, my dear. You are free to remain up here if you like. But I warn you. This will not be pleasant."

"Am I also free to place a wager?"

Strang smiled. "Why, certainly. Whatever amount you want to bet, I will cover. But I should point out that while I appreciate your confidence in me, it really is not necessary."

"Oh, I do not want to bet on you," Keanuenueokalani said. "I want to bet on him." She pointed at Fargo.

The sailors had been quietly talking and joking among themselves, but suddenly, to a man, they fell silent.

"What did you say, my dear?" Strang asked, although he had to have heard her perfectly well.

"I want to bet on Fargo. Would fifty dollars be too much?"

A red tinge spread from Strang's thick neck to his hairline. "Why would you want to bet against the man you have agreed to marry? Or is your affection fickle?"

Kean laughed pleasantly. "Didn't you tell me once that you love to challenge yourself, to push your mind and your body? Perhaps my betting on him will make him try that much harder, and you will have the challenge you want."

"Your logic runs in contrary channels," Strang said. "But to humor you, I will put fifty dollars on him in your behalf."

"How very courteous of you," Kean said, smiling sweetly.

Fargo wondered what she was up to. Her plan called for her to win Strang's confidence and convince him she truly wanted to marry him. By betting against him, no matter how she sugarcoated it, she was bound to make Strang suspicious.

The crew appeared flabbergasted. "Did we hear aright, Captain?" Berm asked. "You are betting against yourself?"

"To please my betrothed," Strang said in a surly manner.

The sailors exchanged glances. Greedy glances, spawned by an idea that had occurred to many of them, and which the first mate gave voice to. "Are you willing to give odds, sir?"

"I don't see why I should."

Berm did not let it rest. "Begging the captain's pardon, but you said yourself that Fargo doesn't stand a chance against you. That being so, why not give odds of two to one or three to one so more of us will bet on him?"

"I see what your game is. You want me to give odds so you need only place a small wager on him, and in the unlikely event he wins, your small wager will bring you more than if you bet on me."

"Then the answer is no," Berm said. "That's all right, Captain. We would not want to take advantage of you."

All Strang had to do was keep quiet and that would be the end of it. But to a man like him, a man who took pride in being better and tougher and meaner than those under him, that would not do. "I tell you what, First Mate. Two to one I accept. Provided no one bets more than my bride-to-be."

The crew huddled to discuss it. The outcome: nearly

everyone bet five to ten dollars on Fargo. Only Collins and Wells bet only on their captain.

Theodore Strang observed the proceedings with an aloof air, as if it was of no consequence. But when the betting was over and Gliss announced that two hundred and fifty dollars was riding on Fargo's shoulders, Strang came over to Fargo and stated in a low tone so only Fargo heard, "The wagers change everything."

"In what way?" Fargo asked. He had an inkling but he wanted to hear it from Strang.

"Forget what I said about going easy on you. I am going to pound you into the deck. If in the bargain I break a few bones, so much the better."

12

The *Poseidon* rolled slightly with the swell of the sea. Fargo had become so accustomed to the motion of the deck that it would not be a factor. What *would* be a factor was the condition of his body. He was not his sharp-as-a-razor self. He had not been eating enough, and the food he did eat was not the kind of food he was used to. He had not been sleeping well, either. Added up, he was out of shape and tired, and pitted against a man who was a solid block of muscle. It did not bode well.

But Fargo would not pass up a chance to repay some of the pain and punishment he had endured. For two weeks now he had been held against his will. Shackled like a criminal, or a slave. He hated it. He hated it to the core of his being. All his adult life he had roamed where whim took him. All his adult life he had been as free as a proverbial bird. Now here he was, held captive, powerless to exercise that freedom. Every time his leg irons had rattled he was reminded of the fact. It stoked his anger, kept him good and mad, so that now, with the leg irons off and Theodore Strang limbering up for their clash, he wanted nothing more in all the world than to smash Strang's face in.

The first mate came to the center of the circle. "Gents," he said with a grin, "the usual rule applies. And that rule is that there aren't any rules. The fight goes until one of you gives up or has stopped breathing. Any questions?" He looked at Fargo when he asked.

Fargo shook his head. He raised his fists and set himself.

"Good," Berm said. "Then we are about ready."

"I have something to say," Strang declared, and raked his crew with a look that suggested he was not at all pleased with them. "It probably goes without saying but I will say it anyway." He paused. "No one is to interfere. No matter what happens, you are to stay out of this. He can inflict as much harm on me as he is capable of."

Fargo was under no illusions about who would inflict the most. His only hope was to strike first and strike hard, and after that to slow the pace of the fight by staying out of reach.

Strang was gazing at the quarterdeck.

Keanuenueokalani smiled encouragement and called out, "Luck to you!" Fargo noticed that she was not looking at Strang when she said it. She could be saying it to him. But Strang apparently did not notice.

"Thank you, my dear. I will not disappoint you. I promise."

"You never disappoint me, Theodore," Kean said. "You always do exactly what I expect you to do."

That could be taken two ways but it satisfied Strang, who turned and raised his thick arms in a boxing stance. "Whenever you are ready, First Mate, you may commence."

Berm skipped back to the ring of eager onlookers, exclaiming, "Start slugging! And may the toughest bastard win!"

Fargo assumed Strang would box. Strang had his fists up, so it seemed only natural. But it was a ruse. Strang advanced, took two short steps, and suddenly lowered his arms, bellowed like a bull, and charged, his arms spread wide to grip and grapple.

Fargo was taken off his guard. He backpedaled but not quite nimbly enough. A two-ton battering ram, or so it seemed, smashed into his gut and lifted him clean off his feet. Before he could land a blow, he was smashed to the deck and lay with his ears ringing and the masts doing a macabre dance. He braced for more but he was left alone. When, after half a minute, the world steadied and he blinked and looked up, Strang was standing over him, his hands on his hips.

"That was just a taste. On your feet. I never hit a man when he is down, rules or no rules."

Fargo was surprised. He slowly stood, his stomach and hips aflame with pain. He raised his fists but watched for a rush.

Strang raised his own. "Let's test your mettle, shall we?"

It was not as if Fargo had any choice in the matter. He blocked a looping right, dodged a flicked left, avoided an uppercut. The punches were not thrown as fast as he expected them to be, and it was only when he saw the tight smile on Strang's face that he realized Strang was not trying his hardest, and that Strang was toying with him, or testing him, as Strang had put it. It made Fargo madder. He threw a straight arm to Strang's stomach, and remarkably, Strang made no attempt to counter. His fist connected solidly. But it was him, not Strang, who recoiled in pain. It was like hitting a tree.

"If you thought it would be easy, you were mistaken," Strang said. "My reputation is justly earned. When I mentioned that no one has ever beaten me, it was not brag or bluster. It was a fact."

Again Fargo set himself. He resented being talked down to, resented being treated as if he were a weakling.

"Nothing to say? Very well. Have it your way."

Strang waded in and it was all Fargo could do to keep from being battered to a pulp. He blocked. He dodged. He ducked. He did all he could, but some of the punches slipped through, sledgehammer blows that rocked him on his heels or caused him to suck in his breath and choke down gasps of agony. He had never fought anyone who inflicted such brutal punishment.

Unexpectedly, Strang stepped back and studied him. "Is this the best you can do?"

"Go to hell," Fargo said, breaking his long silence.

"I am not trying to provoke you," Strang said. "You seem slow, unfocused. For your own sake I will end this quickly."

"Don't do me any favors."

"That was childish. Evidently I misjudged you. You are not the man I took you for. Very well." Strang's lips compressed and he came in with his clublike arms pumping.

Fargo retreated. He could only go so far before he would back into the sailors. But he was counting on that. When he reached them, they laughed and shoved him toward Strang. He pretended to stumble. Dipping on one knee, he threw his hands toward the deck as if to keep from falling on his face.

Strang stopped. His arms widened slightly.

Fargo's trick had worked. From low down near the deck he swept his fist up in a tight arc that caught Theodore Strang full on the chin. There was a loud *crack* like the crack of a bullwhip and Strang staggered.

The sailors, who had been whooping and hollering and generally having a grand time, stopped their chatter and gawked as they might if the ship had sprouted wings and launched itself into the sky.

"I'll be damned!" one blurted.

Strang shook his head to clear it. He rubbed his jaw, then did the last thing Fargo expected of him. He smiled. "Well done. Very well done, indeed. Perhaps you will be more of a challenge than I thought."

Any elation Fargo felt at finally landing a solid blow was erased by the result. Strang came at him now in somber earnest, every blow deliberate, fighting with the precision of a machine. Fargo was not given a moment's respite. He blocked. He slipped. He swung punches of his own. Only a few of his landed, and when they did, his hand nearly always flared in agony.

The minutes stretched into eternities. Once again Fargo had the impression Strang was dragging it out, either to hurt him or—the thought startled him—maybe to impress Keanuenueokalani.

Fargo dared not glance at the quarterdeck. Any lapse in concentration, however slight, would reap disaster.

Suddenly Strang picked up the pace. Shifting right and left, he threw faster and faster punches.

Avoiding them became impossible. Fargo did the best he could but his sluggish body could not take the strain. He rapidly tired, his stamina a shadow of what it should be. A left cross clipped his chin and he saw stars. A solid right drove at his chest but he sidestepped and was caught on the shoulder hard enough to send him tottering against the sailors. When they pushed him this time, he tripped over his own feet and wound up on his hands and knees. He glanced up, thinking Strang would give him time to rise. A fist mushroomed in front of his face and the next moment he was flat on his belly, barely conscious.

"Get up, damn you!" a seaman shouted.

"We have money riding on you!" bellowed another. "Show us what you're made of! On your feet and whip him!"

In their dismay at the prospect of losing the money they had wagered, the pair had forgotten about Strang. "Who said that?" he demanded. "Barnes, was that you?"

"Not me, Captain, sir. I don't know who it was."

Fargo placed his hands flat on the deck and slowly pushed to his knees. He hurt. God, how he hurt. But he was not about to give up. Strang's back was to him, so Strang did not see him move closer, still on his knees, and cock his right fist. "We are not done yet," he declared.

Captain Strang turned.

No rules, the man had said. So long as Strang fought fair, Fargo was willing to do the same. Not now. Not after Strang hit him when he was down. Fargo drove his fist into Strang's groin, into where it would hurt a man the most.

Strang grunted. For a few seconds, he stared down in disbelief, then he doubled over, sputtering and gasping, and clutched himself.

Marshaling all his strength, Fargo unleashed an upper-cut. He hurt his hand again but he also jolted Strang onto his heels, and that was worth any pain. The whoops and yips of the sailors seemed to shake the masts.

Strang was red in the face, as much from rage as from the blow below his belt. With a struggle he straightened, bunched his huge fists, and roared, "So this is how it is?"

A hush fell.

"Some of you have sailed with me many a year," Strang said bitterly. "Yet you side with this landlubber for a few paltry dollars. Is this the sum of our toil and sweat? All you hooligans care about is the money?"

"It's nothing personal, sir," an older crewman made bold to reply.

"Like hell it isn't!" Strang thundered. "I would be less offended if you were to shove my head up a whale's ass." Glowering, he pointed at several of them. "You and you and you! Have I ever treated any of my ship's company with a lack of respect? Have I ever punished for the sake of punishing? Deprived anyone of food or drink? Yet look at how you mistreat me. Look at the lack of respect I am shown."

"You make more of this than there is, sir," Berm said apologetically. "There isn't a man jack here who doesn't regard you as the finest captain he has ever served under."

"Liar," Strang said. "Once I would have believed you. But now I see through your deceptions." He had recovered enough to remove his hands from his groin. "As for you," he growled at Fargo, "I mean to stomp you into the deck. No more holding back."

And just like that, Strang attacked. He flicked a punch and as he did he flicked a leg, too, and nearly shattered Fargo's kneecap. As it was, Fargo narrowly leaped aside, only to receive a backhand across the face that left his lower lip bleeding.

Strang came on. Not in a boxing stance, or with his arms spread wide as a wrestler would do. He simply stalked forward, an unstoppable juggernaut bent on destruction.

Fargo hit at the bigger man's face, at his throat, at his chest. None landed. He kicked at Strang's knee and involuntarily yelped when Strang seized his foot and gave his leg a vicious wrench. A twig caught in a gale, he was flung against the sailors, bowling a half dozen over. An elbow glanced off his ribs. A foot scraped his midriff. Then he was out of the tangle and backing toward the bulwark.

Barely breaking stride, Captain Strang lumbered toward him, a great white whale who would not be denied.

Fargo had been lucky so far but his luck would not hold forever. Sooner or later Strang would back him into a corner, and that would be that. Better, he reasoned, to take the fight to Strang than wait for that to happen. Crouching, he tensed his legs and, when Strang was near enough, launched himself at Strang's shins, seeking to bowl Strang over as he had bowled over the sailors. But where the sailors were reeds and willows, Strang was a redwood. Slamming into his legs was the same as slamming into twin trees.

Fargo's entire side exploded in torment. Iron fingers clamped onto his arm and leg. Before he could even attempt to break free, he was bodily swung into the air, over Strang's head, and held there, as helpless as an infant.

"So much for your paltry wagers!" Strang snarled at his men. "As I dash this fool to the deck, so do I dash your disrespect in your wretched faces!"

Fargo envisioned the result, envisioned having half the bones in his body broken. In a frantic bid to save himself, he threw himself from side to side and forward and back. He did not really think it would work but Strang teetered, nearly losing his grip. Instantly, Fargo kicked and pushed and heaved, and succeeded in tearing loose. He fell, felt his shoulder bump something, and continued to fall.

A shriek that could only come from a female throat pierced the air.

By rights Fargo should have come down hard on the

deck, but it was not unyielding wood he struck. He hit back-first, and was enveloped in wetness and cold. Belatedly, shock coursed through him.

He had fallen over the side.

He was in the sea.

Ten feet down. Fifteen. Fargo felt himself slow and immediately stroked for the paler water above. He broke the surface, his eyes stinging, and saw the *Poseidon* twenty yards away and swiftly widening the gulf. He could not hope to catch her but he swam after her anyway, conscious of figures lining the rail and of shouts. Their cries were a jumble of sounds.

Then one word eclipsed the rest. A word that would send a shiver down the spine of any mariner, or anyone else, for that matter.

That word was *shark*.

Fargo looked over his shoulder.

A large dorsal fin and a tail fin were cleaving the sea toward him.

13

"Swim!" someone yelled.

Fargo did. He swam for all he was worth, his arms and legs churning, but no matter how fast he swam he could not outrace the voracious denizen of the sea. It seemed like no time at all when suddenly the fin was to his right, sweeping around him. The shark was circling as a prelude to attacking.

Fargo stopped swimming. He wished he had his Arkansas toothpick. He could at least get in a few licks before he was torn to pieces.

Up close, the dorsal fin was huge. The shark must be enormous. Twenty feet or more. Fargo watched it curve around him to the other side. There was a continuous soft swish of water as the fin split the surface.

Fargo had no idea what kind of shark it was. He did not know enough about them. He did remember Collins mentioning once that white sharks, tiger sharks, and hammerheads were especially feared by sailors, as all liked to dine on humans.

The shark completed its circle and started another.

Fargo did not take his eyes off it. The situation reminded him of the time a winter-starved pack of ravenous wolves had circled his camp around and around, although they never attacked. His campfire had kept them at bay. But he had no way of keeping this shark at bay. It bore home the fact that he was as out of his element as he could be. He knew the creatures of the mountains and the prairie as well as he knew himself, and could cope with them in a variety of ways. But a shark? In the sea? He stood a snowball's chance in hell.

The dorsal fin came closer on its second pass. Behind it a goodly distance was the tail.

Fargo made out the vague grayish mass of the body underneath. The snout was broad and blunt. It might be a trick of the light but he would swear there were white spots on its back.

Suddenly the shark went under.

His skin crawling, Fargo peered into the water. But he could not see his own feet, let alone the fierce marauder about to separate them and the rest of his legs from his body. He swallowed, or tried to, his mouth so dry it hurt. This was it, he thought. A strange way for him, of all people, to die. In the mountains, yes. On the prairie, yes. But in the middle of the ocean? He never expected his life to end like this.

Something scraped his left foot.

Stifling a cry, Fargo brought his legs up close to his chest. He thought he glimpsed spots but he could not be sure.

The warmth of the sun, the cold of the water, the caress of the air on his face—all Fargo's sensations were intensified, as if, in his final moments, he was experiencing things more keenly than ever before. He wondered if that was typical when someone was about to die.

The shark was taking its sweet time.

The wait was almost unendurable. Every nerve in Fargo's body tingled with the expectation of feeling razor teeth shear into his flesh. "Where are you?" he asked aloud, and promptly clamped his mouth shut.

Then he saw them. The white spots on an impossibly huge back, rising out of the depths toward him. He braced himself and balled his fists to go down swinging, if nothing else.

A new sound intruded. The chock of oars in their locks. He looked up and was never so relieved in his life. The *Poseidon* had lowered a boat to retrieve him, and it was almost to him. He glanced down. The white dots were fading as the great shark dived. He thought the boat had scared it off, and he smiled and whooped. Then he realized the sailors in the boat were laughing, some of them laughing so hard they were bent over the oars.

The first mate was in the bow. He was laughing, too. He signaled for the men to stop rowing and leaned down, offering his hand. "Up you come, landlubber. That is, if you are done with your swim."

Fargo did not find it amusing. He did not find it amusing at all. As he slid over the side, wet and weary, he said to their laughing faces, "You can all go to hell."

"You don't understand," Berm said.

"What is there to savvy?" Fargo snapped. "You think it's funny, that damn shark almost eating me."

"That would be a feat," the first mate said, and laughed harder. At length he contained himself enough to say, "It was a whale shark."

"A what?"

"A whale shark, landlubber, and a small one, at that. It couldn't eat you if it wanted to. Its mouth is like a sieve. They feed on small fish and the like."

"A whale shark," Fargo said. He half expected Berm was making it up until Wells cackled and slapped his thigh.

"The look on your face! Over a whale shark! I'll be telling my grandkids this one."

Fargo started to shiver. He hugged his legs to him, missing more than ever the forests and grasslands he called home.

"You were lucky it was only a whale shark," the first mate remarked. "If it had been a great white, we wouldn't be having this talk."

"I suppose you expect me to thank you for coming to get me."

"Not at all," Berm said. "We were only following orders. The captain told us to fetch you, so here we are."

The men applied the oars and the boat began its loop back toward the *Poseidon*.

Berm was unusually talkative. "That was some fight you had. I wouldn't have lasted half as long as you did."

"I'm surprised Strang bothered to send you after me," Fargo said.

"Why wouldn't he? He's tough, but he's not cruel. Besides, you have your shanghai to serve, and you have only just begun."

"Don't remind me."

The first mate shrugged. "It's what you get for sticking your big nose where it did not belong."

"A woman was in trouble. I helped her."

"Justify it any way you want, but you brought this down on your own head," Berm said without sympathy. "I must admit, you have handled it better than most. Who knows? Give us another year or two and we might make a sailor out of you."

"I would rather have land under me," Fargo said. "You can keep the sea."

"Gladly." The first mate gazed out over the briny blue-green. "I love the ocean. I love everything about it. I was raised on Nantucket, and whales and whaling are all anyone ever talks about. My father was a whaler and I followed in his footsteps. I have never regretted it, either."

"Shanghaiing people is wrong."

Berm looked at him. "We're back to that, are we? For your information, our captain isn't like some, who shanghai half their crew to save the expense of paying them. He only does it now and again, and only to punish some dunderhead, like you."

"You like Strang, don't you?"

"What's not to like?" the first mate rejoined. "He's as competent a captain as there is anywhere. He is hard on us, sure, but only because if he wasn't, we would slack off, and we know it as well as he does. But I tell you this. When a tempest is blowing or some other calamity rears its head, there is no one on this earth I would rather serve under than Captain Theodore Strang."

"Hear, hear," one of the rowers said.

"He's the best, our captain," Wells declared. "And we would whip any scurvy rat who said different."

"This saint of yours is forcing a woman to marry him against her will," Fargo said.

Berm lost some of his good humor. "We never said he's a saint. He is as human as you and me. As for the female, our captain saved her father and the old man offered him anything he wanted. He happened to want her."

This was news to Fargo. "Saved the father how?"

"There was a storm. Not a typhoon, mind, but a bad one. We had left Honolulu and were putting out to open sea when it swept in on us. The captain decided to wait it out in a lagoon. We were about to drop anchor when the lookout spotted a canoe with some natives in it. They were trying to make shore but the canoe capsized. All of them drowned except one. The girl's father. We threw a rope to him and hauled him up."

"And he was so grateful he offered his daughter to Strang," Fargo said skeptically.

"Not right off, no. He was grateful, yes, and told the captain he could have anything he wanted in return. Captain Strang wasn't all that interested until after the storm was over and we lowered a boat and rowed the native in. The rest of the villagers came out to meet us. That was when the captain saw Kean for the first time, and was smitten."

"Kean wasn't smitten with him—" Fargo began, and bit off the rest. He almost let slip how much she despised Strang.

"Not then, but women are fickle. After slipping off the ship and leading us a merry chase in San Francisco, now she decides she wants to be his bride, after all."

"Will all of you be at the wedding?"

"The captain hasn't told us yet," Berm replied. "I imagine some will have to stay on board. That includes you." He smiled. "I expect to be invited. It should be a fine celebration. Those islanders do it right. A lot of food and a lot to drink, and of course their women. A willing bunch. Not as willing as in the old days, but there are plenty as like a tumble as not."

"The old days?"

"Before they got religion. To them making love was as natural as breathing. Hell, those girls would swim out to the ship for the privilege. Then the damned missionaries started in on their souls and got those Hawaiian women so they wouldn't part their grass skirts. A lot of them, anyway. There are always those who like to do it, perdition or no perdition."

This was the most the first mate had spoken to him since he was shanghaied. Fargo pumped the information well with, "What do the Hawaiian men think of their women cavorting with sailors?"

"They didn't seem to mind much back in the old days," Berm related. "Now some do. But with them it's not religion—it's politics. Now that they have a government and are a kingdom, they think they are the equal of us whites. Uppity cusses, but what can you do?"

"Ever been to a Hawaiian wedding? What is it like?"

"Can't say as I have, no," Berm admitted. "But the captain was saying as how he expects it to last a couple of days. There is some pagan nonsense to go through, and a feast."

"Will a man of the cloth be there?"

Berm laughed. "Not if the captain can help it. That way, if he decides later he can live without her, he can cast Kean off without having to worry about the legality. The captain has it all worked out."

"He thinks of everything," Fargo said dryly.

"That he does. Yet another reason we sign up with him voyage after voyage. We're in good hands."

The boat was approaching the *Poseidon*. At the rail, conspicuous by his size was Theodore Strang. His hat, shirt, and coat were on, his big hands clasped behind his back, as was his custom. He barked orders for his men to be ready to raise the boat and they scampered to obey.

"Another thing you should know," the first mate said to Fargo as the boat came alongside the ship. "We wouldn't take it kindly if you tried to hurt our captain. Oh, we cheered you on when a few dollars were at stake, but we didn't really want you to do him harm. Keep that in mind."

Fargo was glad when he was finally on board. Collins was waiting for him, and started right in with, "You have a lot of work to do before you can call it a day. Back to mopping, and be quick about it."

"Hold up there, Third Mate," Strang intervened. He regarded Fargo with what might pass for genuine concern. "I want you to know I did not throw you overboard deliberately. I slipped, and over the side you went."

"Does it matter?" Fargo asked. Nothing the man could say would make him think better of him.

"It does to me," Strang said. "You have earned my respect."

"I can't say the same."

Strang frowned. "I can't blame you for feeling as you do. I would feel the same, were you in my shoes and I in yours. But that does not mean we have to be enemies, does it?"

"You've had me in leg irons the past two weeks," Fargo reminded him. "You figure it out."

"The shackles stay off," Strang said, adding, "so long as you behave, that is."

"Don't hold your breath waiting for me to thank you."

Strang made that *tsk-tsk* sound. "Why throw my kindness in my face? I could make things a lot worse for you. A lot worse," he stressed.

"Want me to have him tied to the mast and whipped?" Collins asked.

"Belay talk like that," Strang snapped. To Fargo he said, "I can see my efforts are wasted. You won't ever forgive me for forcing you into sea service." Wheeling, he departed with, "Permit him ten minutes to rest from his swim, Third Mate. Then you may put him to work."

"Aye, aye, Captain." Collins did not sound happy about it. Muttering, he went forward.

Fargo found himself alone. Wearily leaning on the rail, he ran a hand through his still-wet hair.

"Don't ever scare me like that again."

At Kean's whisper, Fargo smiled. "I'll try not to."

103

"I am serious," Keanuenueokalani said. "Without you, my plan will not work. I will be forced to marry that monster. Little does he suspect I would slit my wrists rather than submit."

"Submit to him or to any man?" Fargo ogled her body, and winked.

Kean laughed, caught herself, and laughed some more. "Are you saying you would like to have your way with me if you could?"

It had been two weeks since Fargo was with Molly, two weeks and a lot of seafaring miles. He was honest with Kean. "I would eat you alive."

14

The Kingdom of Hawaii.

A patch of green rose out of the sea, swelling and growing until it took on the dimensions of a large island: Oahu. Essentially two mountain ranges with a broad valley in between, its fertile soil was the Kingdom's food basket. More Hawaiians lived on Oahu than on any of the other islands.

Shortly after the lookout called out, "Land, ho!" Keanuenueokalani came hurriedly on deck and stood in the bow, gazing yearningly at her home. Strang came up with her, but after a while left her to attend to his duties.

Fargo waited a few minutes, then drifted toward her. Collins was busy elsewhere and he had been left on his own. Careful that no one overheard, he remarked, "I bet you are happy to be back."

"You have no idea," Kean said softly, her eyes moist. "I have never been so happy in all my life."

It had taken the *Poseidon* slightly over four weeks to make the crossing. From what Fargo understood, that was typical. Some ships could do it in less, but they did not stop to kill and butcher whales along the way.

"I have missed my home, my people, so very much," Kean went on. "I yearn for those I love, to have my mother hold me in her arms, to see my father again."

"Even after he let Strang take you?"

"He could not stop it," Kean said, and sighed. "You see, he was horrified when Strang asked for me. When he promised Strang anything he owned for saving his life, he never meant that Strang could take one of his daughters. He asked that Strang take something else, anything else, but Strang insisted. I was all Strang wanted. He would settle for nothing less. They talked for several days but my father would not give in, so Strang came in the night with some of his men and took me."

Fargo listened with keen interest.

"I was scared, so very scared. I feared Strang would force himself on me the moment we were on the ship, but he did not touch me. To my great surprise, he said he wanted that we do it right. His exact words. He wanted me to care for him as he claimed he cared for me. That is the only thing that saved me." Kean stopped. She trembled slightly and gripped the rail. "I was honest with him. I told him I could never love him. I told him that if he did force himself on me, I would be his in body only, never in my heart or my head."

"How did he take that?" Fargo asked.

"Better than I thought he would. He said that in time I would come to care for him. He said he would be patient with me, and that he was taking me to see the sights of San Francisco. To impress me, I think. But I escaped from the ship, and the rest you know."

The hiss of spray off the prow was punctuated by the shrill cries of birds that were wheeling over the waves to the northwest.

"We will make land within the hour," Fargo predicted. "Has Strang said yet whether he will put in at Honolulu?" The American consul was there, and if Fargo could reach him, he could put an end to all this.

"It is my understanding he will not," Kean answered. "He would rather not deal with government officials if he can help it. He intends to slip quietly in, marry me, and slip quietly out to sea again."

"He is not going to let me be at the wedding," Fargo mentioned.

"As we expected," Keanuenueokalani said.

"Will you be able to do your part?"

"I will try my utmost. He keeps the key in a pocket of his coat and never takes it out except to use it."

"A lot depends on getting that key," Fargo noted.

"I know, I know." Kean looked at him. "No matter what happens, I want to thank you for all you have tried to do. I am sorry I brought so much hardship down on your shoulders."

"I have been through worse."

Kean started to reach out to touch him but dropped her arm to her side before anyone could notice. "Promise me you will not let yourself be hurt. I would not want that on my conscience as well."

"What will be, will be," was Fargo's outlook. "But don't blame yourself if it does." He smiled encouragingly. "I may not harpoon my own whales but I do shoot my own buffalo."

Kean smiled. "If we live through this, I would take it as an honor to show you around the island."

"If we live through this, I would like that." Fargo imagined how she would look without the dress, imagined her ripe, young body under his. The ship and the sea blurred in the heat of his imaginary passion, and he paid for his lapse with a sharp jab in the back.

"What the hell are you doing?" Collins demanded. "Bothering the captain's woman?"

Keanuenueokalani came to Fargo's rescue. "He was as polite as could be. I was telling him about my people and my home, is all."

Collins harrumphed and gave Fargo a push. "The captain wants to see you in his quarters. Get below, and don't dawdle."

Fargo could not begin to guess why. At his knock, Strang bid him enter, and indicated he should take a chair across from the teak desk where Strang sat writing in a ledger. Fargo complied. The scratch of the pen was the only sound in the cabin until Strang set the pen down and leaned back, his chair creaking.

"Congratulations. You have survived your first month at sea."

"Break out a bottle of whiskey and we will celebrate."

"Your sarcasm is duly noted. But your time on board has not been all that terrible, has it?"

"I won't even answer that," Fargo said in disgust.

"Very well. But I was hoping you had accepted the inevitable by now. Defiance will not make the next two years and eleven months any easier."

"Listen to yourself," Fargo snapped. "You hold a man against his will and expect him to lick your boots."

"That is not it," Strang said. "That is not it at all." He sighed. "Life is about learning to make the best of situations as they arise. You must learn to make the best of yours."

"If you believe that, you're insane."

Strang arched an eyebrow. "That was rather childish, don't you think? All things considered, I have treated you decently. But given your attitude, you will appreciate why I do what I must." With that, he clapped his hands loudly, twice.

The door opened and in filed the first mate along with Wells and two other sailors. The first mate held a familiar object. He came over next to Fargo's chair and rattled the chain.

"Remember these, landlubber?"

Berm would never know how close he came to Fargo punching his teeth in. "So much for being treated decently."

Strang did not rise to the insult. "While I have given you the run of the ship while we have been at sea, and permitted the leg irons to be removed, you will submit to being shackled whenever we make landfall. The temptation might prove too much, and I would spare myself the bother of having to hunt you down."

"Stretch out your legs," Berm directed. "If you don't, I'll have these others hold you down."

Fargo did as he was told. Resisting was pointless. He would bide his time a while yet. Then, if everything went according to plan, he intended to bother the hell out of the *Poseidon*'s captain and crew.

"Your legs irons will be removed once we are out on the open sea again," Strang informed him.

Berm sank to his knees to do the deed. "Begging your pardon, sir, but you are too nice to this monkey. Were it me, I wouldn't ever take the leg irons off."

"He has not given us any trouble, has he?" Strang rejoined. "Until he does, he will be rewarded with a limited amount of freedom."

The remark seared Fargo like a red-hot branding iron, seared him deep inside. Fury boiled, and it was only with the greatest effort that he contained his seething emotions and hid his rage. He adopted a poker face and sat there unruffled as the leg irons were once again clamped fast.

"There," Berm said, giving the chain a yank. "He won't dare try anything with these on."

"You and the others may leave us, First Mate," Strang commanded. "Make ready for landfall. Tell whoever is in the crow's nest to keep a sharp eye out for the lagoon. The inlet is narrow, and if he does not stay alert, we could sail right by it."

"Aye, aye, Captain."

After the door closed, Strang shifted his chair so he could gaze out over the ocean. "Do you mind if we talk a bit?"

"You're asking *me*?" Fargo said.

"I feel the need, and there is no one else. My men are not all that sentimental."

"And you are?"

Strang glanced around. "Do me the courtesy of sheathing your claws for a few minutes. Can you do that much?"

"This after you clamp me in leg irons again?" Fargo said. "You are as fickle as the weather."

"Not so, frontiersman. I always know what I am about. For instance, I am about to take a step many men take, and I warrant most feel the way I do. Nervous. Uneasy. The prospect of taking a woman for my wife does not sit easily on my brow. Nor, I would guess, does it sit easily on the lovely brow of my intended."

Here was a side to Strang that Fargo had not expected. It ruined the image Fargo had of him: a coldhearted monster with no regard for anyone but himself. "I don't want to hear this."

"Indulge me, please. I have no one else to talk to."

Fargo said nothing.

Evidently taking that as agreement, Strang continued. "I never thought this would happen to me, of all people. Women have never held much interest for me. They are weak, mewing creatures, with only two purposes in life. One is to pleasure men. The other is to have babies. Beyond that, there is nothing they can do that a man can't do as well or better."

Fargo relaxed. This was more like the old Strang. "I like pleasure as much as the next man, but you're wrong. There is more to women than that. A lot more."

"In what regard? They chatter. They pout. They manipulate a man until they have him under their thumb."

"Women can be playful. They can be fun. Sure, they're moody, but men are moody, too. Only women are more honest about it. They don't hide their moods as men do." Fargo paused. "If that's how you feel about them, why in hell are you marrying Kean?"

"Because she is the one woman I do not feel that way about," Strang replied. "I can't explain it, other than that, from the moment I set eyes on her, I have wanted her as I have never wanted anyone. She is different from all the rest. She is quiet and levelheaded, sweet and innocent. I look at her and I see purity. I look at her and I ache, I want her so much."

Again Fargo had to resort to a poker face. It occurred to him that Theodore Strang was one of those men who had no understanding whatsoever of what women were about.

"I have never felt like this. I tried to deny my urges but I can't. I have to have her. But I couldn't bring myself to simply throw her on my bed and have my way. It is what most of my crew would do. Even the married ones dally with the island girls. Not that I condemn them, you understand. I have just never felt the need to indulge."

Fargo had listened to enough. He was going to go whether Strang liked it or not. He tensed his arms to push up out of the chair.

"May I ask you a personal question?"

God, no, Fargo thought.

"Have you ever been in love?" Strang turned, his walrus features etched in earnest appeal. "Have you ever felt like I do?"

"There have been a few women—" Fargo began, and let it go at that. He was not comfortable baring his soul to a man he might have to kill.

"Were they all you thought about, day and night? Did you see their reflections in the mirror when you washed? Did you see their faces in the clouds above you?"

"You have it bad," Fargo said.

"I do, don't I? I am acting as if I am a love-struck sixteen-year-old, but I can't help myself. By all that is holy, I can't stop it."

Fargo did not know what to say to that, so he did not say anything.

For a considerable while Strang, too, was silent, his brow knit, his chin bowed. "I suppose," he said at last, "I am behaving like a horse's ass. Forgive my indulgence. It was wrong of me to inflict myself on you."

"I didn't mind," Fargo lied.

"It is all moot, anyway," Strang said. "Today we arrive at the village. Tomorrow or the day after the ceremony will be held. The day after that, I set sail for the South Seas and a season of whaling."

"Are you taking Kean with you?"

"Do you honestly think I would leave my new bride behind?" Strang was reverting to his cold, abrupt self.

"Isn't it bad luck to have a woman on board?" Fargo reminded him. "Your men say that on a passenger ship it was acceptable but on a whaler it was not."

"The men might think so but I don't share their silly superstitions," Strang declared.

"You would risk a mutiny?"

"I would risk the fires of hell itself," Strang replied. "Once she is mine, I will no longer be denied. Not by her, not by my crew, not by God Almighty." He turned his back. "Our talk is over. Go find the third mate. Tell him I said you are to help lower the anchor."

Fargo was somber as he climbed to the deck. Theodore Strang did not know it yet, but the wedding might not take place. Not if he had anything to do with it. He had put up with a lot the past month. Soon, very soon, he would show the captain and crew of the *Poseidon* that they had made the biggest mistake of their lives when they shanghaied him.

Soon, very soon, it would be time to spill blood.

15

Hawaii was beautiful. Fargo could think of no other way to describe it. Of all the places he had been—and his wanderlust had taken him practically everywhere west of the Mississippi River—Hawaii dazzled like no other. The towering Rockies with their mantles of snow were magnificent in their way, and the endless rolling prairies with their shimmering grass and spectacular wildflowers were a sight to behold, but neither compared to the spectacular wonder that was Hawaii.

From the deck of the *Poseidon* Fargo stared, and marveled.

The lagoon was the Garden of Eden all over again. The rich blue of the water, water so clear he could see every bright pebble and every flash of brilliantly colored fish, was bluer than any high country lake he had ever set eyes on. Thanks to the sheltering arms of the inlet, the lagoon was perfectly still, virtually a blue mirror, roughly oval in shape and fringed by sand that appeared to be almost white.

Beyond reared hills that blended into the Koolau Range. Every square foot was covered with a riot of vegetation of all kinds, many of which Fargo had never seen before and had no name for. Tropical plants and trees found nowhere on the mainland. He spotted several birds, their plumage as colorful as their surroundings, but could not identify them. Flowers were abundant.

Between the beach and the hills stood the village. A substantial settlement, judging by the number of huts.

Most were on the scale of a log cabin, a few larger, built mainly of grass and rushes. Fully sixty near-naked bronzed natives gathered to greet the boat that put out from the *Poseidon* with Captain Strang and a dozen heavily armed crew members. Keanuenueokalani sat in the bow, next to Strang, who stood with his hands on a pair of Remington revolvers.

The boat came to rest near a long line of canoes. Much larger than the canoes used by whites and red men on the mainland, these were seaworthy craft, able to travel from island to island.

Fargo half hoped the Hawaiians would pounce on Strang and the sailors and take them captive or wipe them out. Strang, after all, had spirited Keanuenueokalani away in the dark of night. But it was not to be. After a heavyset Hawaiian and Strang talked awhile, the heavyset man, apparently a leader or chief of some kind, addressed the rest of his people in their own tongue, and to Fargo's disgust the natives gave the sailors a warm reception and ushered them into the village. He lost sight of Kean and Strang when they entered the largest of the huts.

"I wish I was with them instead of having to stay on board with you." Collins had come up behind Fargo unnoticed, and leaned on the bulwark. "Berm and Gliss get to have a grand old time, but not me."

"You don't need to stay on my account," Fargo told him.

"Yes, I do, and you damn well know it," Collins said resentfully. "The captain gave me specific orders. I'm stuck nursemaiding you, damn it, when I could be fondling one of those island beauties."

A second boatload of sailors, bristling with weapons, was waiting to go ashore. They laughed and beamed when the first mate appeared on the strip of sand and beckoned, the signal for them to lower a boat.

That left Collins and three sailors. He swore and cast spiteful glances at Fargo.

The sun was an hour above the western horizon. That hour would go slowly, Fargo mused, anxious to make

114

his move. But he must wait for darkness. Under cover of night it would be easier, if only slightly less dangerous.

Collins was squinting at him. "What was that business between the girl and you right before she climbed in the boat?"

"Business?" Fargo stalled. No one else had paid much attention. Strang had been looking the other way.

"She gave you a hug and held your hands and said something I couldn't hear," Collins said. "What was that about?"

"I wished her the best and she thanked me."

"With a hug?" Collins was skeptical. "She was too damn friendly, if you ask me. I should have told the captain but I didn't think of it until he was under way."

"It doesn't matter now, does it?" Fargo asked, his tone as calm as he could make it. He must not let the other suspect the excitement simmering inside of him. If all went well he would soon be rid of his shackles.

"I guess not," Collins conceded. "But I still think it was strange of her. The two of you haven't hardly talked the whole trip, that I know of, yet she treated you like you were her lover."

"I wouldn't mind that one bit," Fargo said.

The third mate allowed himself a laugh. "Nor would I. She's a ripe one, that girl. Makes your mouth water to look at her. Of course, if you ever tell the captain I said that, I'll deny it and slit your throat some night when it suits me.

"Why would I tell?" Fargo said. "He's as liable to knock me down as you."

"That he is," Collins agreed. "Theodore Strang can be a hellion when his dander is up." He started to walk off. "I'm going below. You stay up here. And don't try anything. The lookout will give a holler, and it will just be too bad for you."

Fargo glanced up at the crow's nest. The lookout was watching the village. Strang had told the man to keep a sharp watch on the boats. The other two sailors were on the quarterdeck.

It seemed to take forever for the golden orb to disappear over the rim of the world. Gradually the glare of day softened to the gray of twilight and then the ink of night.

The lights of cooking fires and torches blossomed in the village.

Fargo was ready. Another glance at the crow's nest assured him it was too dark for the lookout to see him. He started to turn, and inwardly swore.

Collins had come up from below. He was walking a little unsteadily, and he smelled of grog. "Rotten missionaries," he said.

"Who?" Fargo responded.

"Don't your ears work? The missionaries, may they rot in hell. If not for them and their prattle about virtue, some of those pretty Hawaiian girls would have shed their grass skirts and swam out to the ship. That's how it was in the old days."

Fargo pretended to be interested. "You miss the old days, I take it."

"You can bet your last dollar I do," Collins answered. He chuckled. "Every sailor wanted to come to Hawaii back then. The women were willing and there was plenty to eat and drink. It was paradise. Not like it is now. The missionaries have the women thinking their bodies are holy shrines. That it is sinful for a man to touch them."

"Quite a change," Fargo commented.

"Not for the better, either." Collins spat over the side. "Those Bible-thumpers should be boiled in oil for what they did."

"I can help you take your mind off it."

"How?"

Fargo hit him. He swept his fist up from the hip and planted it squarely on the third mate's jaw. Collins staggered but did not go down. It took two more blows, delivered with lightning quickness. Fargo caught him before he fell and lowered him. No outcry came from the crow's nest. The two sailors who had been on the quarterdeck had long since gone below.

Fargo looked at the key in his other hand. The key Keanuenueokalani had slipped to him when she hugged him. Hunkering, he inserted it into the left shackle and twisted. There was a click and the shackle popped open. Careful the chain did not clank or rattle, he set the shackle on the deck. He inserted the key into the other leg iron, and a few seconds later, he was free. He headed aft. He had a lot to do and not a lot of time in which to do it. At any moment one of the sailors might come up and find Collins.

Belowdecks was quiet. Fargo listened but did not hear voices or other sounds that would tell him where the other sailors were. He glided along the shadowed passageway to the door to the captain's cabin. It was unlocked. There was no need for Strang to lock it. His men didn't dare enter his private sanctum without his permission.

The cabinet Fargo wanted, the one Keanuenueokalani had told him about, was in a far corner. She said Strang never locked it, but when Fargo tried to open it, he learned she was mistaken. He tugged in frustration, then drew back his bare foot to kick it. Since that would accomplish nothing other than to hurt his foot, he settled for smacking the cabinet instead. A swift survey of the cabin turned up nothing he could use.

"Damn."

Back in the passage, Fargo moved on cat's feet, aware every second squandered was a second closer to being caught. He tried the first mate's cubby. A large knife interested him but he doubted the blade was strong enough. He needed something heavy, something with heft.

The carpenter's bench rewarded him with a hammer. He raced back to Strang's cabin. Standing in front of the cabinet, he hesitated. What he was about to do would be heard all over the ship. The other sailors would come on the run. But it couldn't be helped. Fargo swung the hammer with all his might. Once, twice, three times, and the wood splintered. Four, five, six times, and he had an opening he could stick his hand through. Seven, eight, nine, and that which he sought was revealed.

Fargo beamed. He was so damned happy, he could

whoop for joy. Strang's spare coat, extra shirts, and two pairs of pants hung from a pole. Piled under them on the bottom of the cabinet were Fargo's hat, his buckskin shirt, and his boots and socks. Next to them lay his curled gun belt with his Colt in the holster and the ankle sheath in which the Arkansas toothpick nestled.

Somewhere in the *Poseidon* someone was shouting.

Quickly, Fargo pulled on his socks and tugged into his boots. He donned his shirt and his hat. He was strapping on the Colt when voices sounded in the passage. He wedged the knife sheath under his belt for the time being and swiftly crossed the cabin. Just as he pressed his back to the bulkhead, the door opened and in rushed the two sailors. Both held knives. They ran past him and stopped when they saw the cabinet.

"What the hell!" one exclaimed. "I knew I heard something."

"It must be the landlubber," the other said. "What do you suppose was in there?"

Sidling to the doorway, Fargo drew his Colt. "Turn around and find out," he suggested.

Both spun. Both froze at sight of the six-shooter.

"Drop the blades."

The two knives clattered down.

"Follow me," Fargo directed, backing out. "Keep your hands where I can see them."

"You can't get away," the scruffier of the pair growled.

"He's right," said the other. "There is nowhere to go except the island. We will hunt you down in no time."

"You can try," Fargo retorted. He came to the first mate's cubby, went another couple of steps, and stopped. "In you go," he said, wagging the Colt.

They didn't argue, the scruffy one remarking, "What good will this do? There's no lock on the door."

"Would you rather I just shoot you?"

"I dare you," the scruffy sailor challenged him. "Fire a shot and the lookout will hear and yell for the captain. How far do you think you will get then?"

"Face the wall."

The instant they turned, Fargo sprang. He smashed

the Colt down on Scruffy's head and then on the other, and both sailors folded. Palming the toothpick, he cut the first mate's blanket into strips. With these he bound and gagged the sailors. Satisfied they would not get loose anytime soon, he hastened up on deck.

The first thing he did was check on the lookout. It was so dark he couldn't see the crow's nest, which meant the lookout couldn't see him, either.

The second thing was to make sure Collins had not revived.

The third thing was to figure out how to reach shore. Fargo could lower a boat but the lookout would hear. He could swim, but he would rather not get his clothes— and the Colt and toothpick—wet. Squatting, he strapped the toothpick to his ankle and was about done when a barrel caught his eye. It was used to collect rainwater. He opened the top, and as he expected, it was empty. They had not had to use it on their crossing.

Rope hanging on a peg from the mizzenmast was the next article he helped himself to. From there he crept aft to the quarterdeck and the stern rail. Looping the rope around the keg, he tied a double knot and slowly lowered the keg until it bobbed on the water. He secured the other end to the metal base of the large lantern that lit the quarterdeck at night but was not lit now. After pulling on the rope a few times to make sure it would hold, he climbed over the side. He slipped as he started down and had to clamp his hands and legs tight to stop. The rope nearly rubbed his palms raw. Taking a deep breath, he slowly descended. The rope swayed and jiggled but he had a firm hold.

The keg, or cask to the seamen, bobbed like an oversized cork. He slid down until his chest was over the top and his legs were dangling. His weight caused the keg to dip but it did not go all the way under. He untied the rope, held on, and kicked.

The beach seemed impossibly far, a pale strip against the backdrop of ebony. Soon he was soaked from the hips down, but he was alive and free and armed, and he was going to stay that way if he had to kill every sailor on the *Poseidon*. He remembered some of them saying these waters were shark-infested. He tried not to think about it but twice he swore something brushed his legs. Each time his breath caught in his throat and he braced for savage bites, but he was not attacked.

Then Fargo was in shallow water. He could stand. Pushing the keg ahead of him, he waded out of the surf and sank to his knees. He was so glad to have solid ground under him again that he almost kissed it. But his joy was short-lived. Once again fate proved fickle.

Footsteps sounded in the sand.

Fargo flattened, his hand swooping to his Colt. If he was caught he would die fighting rather than submit to being shackled again.

A silhouette acquired darkling form. A man was coming slowly along the beach toward him. As yet Fargo could not tell if it was a Hawaiian or a crewman from the *Poseidon*.

Then a gruff voice demanded, "Who's there? I know I heard something." A gun barrel glinted dully in the starlight.

16

The sailor was gazing out across the lagoon at the *Poseidon*. His other hand rested on the hilt of a long knife on his hip.

Fargo crabbed backward into the darkness. He did not want to shoot if he could help it. The shot would bring the others.

"I know I heard something," the sailor repeated. He stopped, then looked down and saw the cask almost at his feet. "What the hell?" he blurted. "How did this get here?"

Fargo could not let the man cry out for Strang. In a twinkling he was off the ground. He slammed the Colt against the man's head twice and left him in a disjointed pile.

The village spread before him. Most of the huts were dark and empty. Most everyone was at the large structure farther in. From it wafted loud voices and laughter. Apparently Strang had been forgiven for spiriting Kean away without her father's consent, and the white men were being welcomed with typical Hawaiian hospitality.

On cat's paws Fargo crept from hut to hut. He was rounding one when, without warning, a woman stepped from the doorway, carrying what appeared to be wreaths of some kind. They nearly collided. Fargo started to reach for her to clamp his hand over her mouth so she would not give him away, but it hit him that she had no idea who he was. For all she knew, he was one of the sailors. His hat was different from theirs, and none of the sailors wore buckskins, but he counted on her not being all that familiar with white ways, and instead of grabbing her, he smiled and said, "Good evening, ma'am."

She gave a start. But at his smile she flashed her teeth and said something in Hawaiian, then hurried past toward the large hut.

Fargo stopped skulking. Thumbs in his gun belt, he sauntered along as if he had every right to be there. He passed two more women, both of whom averted their faces. Working his way to the rear of the large hut, he hunkered. There was no window. Drawing the toothpick, he pried at the grass wall. The little noise he made was drowned out by the boisterous revels inside. Soon he had a crack he could see through. He put his eye to it.

Evidently the Hawaiians had no need for furniture. The hut was empty of everything save people. The floor had been strewn with pebbles and then covered, for the most part, with mats made from some kind of plant. It struck Fargo that, just as the Indian tribes of the plains depended largely on the buffalo for their clothes and dwellings, so, too, did the Hawaiians depend on the rich plant life all around them.

The welcoming celebration was well under way. On one side sat the Hawaiians, on the other side the crew. Smiling women moved among the sailors, refilling drinks. Toward the rear of the hut, quite near to Fargo, seated sideways to him, were Captain Strang and First Mate Berm. Across from them sat Kean, a heavyset Hawaiian Fargo took to be her father, and a woman who might be her mother.

Fargo was surprised that many of the women, like the men, were naked from the waist up. The missionaries had done their best to stamp out the practice, branding it as vile, but old ways died hard, and Kean had told him her people never saw anything unnatural or hideous about the naked human form. It had surprised them considerably that the whites thought nakedness wicked.

The sailors could not disguise their lust. Whatever they were drinking was having the effect liquor would.

Their sweaty faces were aglow with carnal craving. A few practically drooled whenever a woman came close. Plainly, they wanted to indulge their hunger, but just as plainly, they were held in check by the commanding presence of their captain.

Strang had just finishing taking a sip. "Tell your father I thank him for his hospitality," he said to Keanuenueokalani. "I am happy he understands and forgives me."

Kean was the one person in the entire hut who did not share in the general good mood. Frowning, she translated, then patiently listened to her father's response. Her frown deepened. "My father says that you are always welcome in our village, Captain Strang. You saved his life and he is forever in your debt."

"Call me Theodore, remember?" Strang said. "Or Theo, if you wish."

"My father also says that he is pleased you have decided to return and marry me according to our customs."

"How soon can we hold the ceremony? I would like to get it over with tomorrow and be on our way the day after."

Keanuenueokalani put the question to her father. His long reply brought a grin. "Imaikalani says that while he would like to honor your request, what you ask is impossible. A feast must be held, a celebration that all may come and see his daughter wed to the great captain." She said the last two words mockingly.

Strang reddened but controlled his temper.

"It will take time to prepare," Kean went on. "Word must be sent to other villages, and to friends on the other islands. The food must be gathered."

"How much time are we talking about?" Strang asked.

"He says they need a month," Kean said, her grin widening, "but that for you, since he knows you are in a hurry to hunt for whales, he can arrange the ceremony in two weeks."

"That is unacceptable."

Kean put his remark to her father and Imaikalani again went on at some length. "My father says he is sorry you feel this way. But he would like for you to understand that this will be a very special day for him and my mother and our people. No one from our village has ever married a white man before."

"But two weeks—" Strang began.

Unlikely support came from the first mate. "If you don't mind my saying so, sir, the men wouldn't mind."

"I am quite sure they wouldn't," Strang said sternly. "Look at them, with their tongues hanging out."

Keanuenueokalani had more. "My father also wants me to tell you that if you will agree, he will show his gratitude by making it worth your while."

"Worth my while how?" Strang demanded.

"He says that he knows where there is much sandalwood. If you are willing, he will have the young men gather it, and when you are done hunting whales, you can return and load the sandalwood on your ship."

Berm sat up straighter. "There's a lot of money to be had in sandalwood, Captain."

"Do you think I don't know that, First Mate?" Strang snapped. He stared at Imaikalani and rubbed his walrus chin. "The chief might be on to something here. We get the sandalwood for free, sell it at any port along the West Coast, and increase our profits by a third, if not more."

"You agree, then?" Kean asked him.

"Tell your father I will think about it and give him my answer in the morning."

Another exchange between daughter and father resulted in, "My father says to take as long as you want to make up your mind. He says that as our honored guests, he and my mother will do all in their power to make your stay comfortable. With that in mind, he says that you and your men are welcome to sleep in this hut if you like."

"Tell him I am grateful," Captain Strang said. "My men and I, though, will spend the night on the ship." He paused. "You are to accompany us."

"Why?"

"Because I say so."

Kean could not hide her anger. "I would rather stay with my parents. I have not seen them in months."

"I sympathize, my dear," Strang said. "Truly, I do. But it would be stupid of me, would it not, to leave you here, knowing full well that when I return in the morning, you will have snuck off in the middle of the night to hide in the hills until I give up looking and sail away?"

Her mother spoke, then her father. Kean replied, and relayed to Strang, "My parents are not pleased. They do not understand why you will not let me stay. Should I tell them the truth?"

"The truth, my dear?" Strang said. "The truth is that you agreed to become my wife. I accepted your word and brought you here. Are you suggesting you do not intend to honor it?" When Kean did not answer he leaned toward her. "I would hate to think that was the case. I would hate to find out that you tricked me into coming."

Kean did not respond.

"Because if you did, if you plan to appeal to your parents for help, there is something you should be aware of. Mark my next words well." Strang was smiling but the smile did not reach his eyes. "I will wipe out this entire village before I let you slip through my fingers. Every last man, woman, and child. In fact, unless you tell your parents that you *want* to go back to the ship with me tonight, I will give the order and my men will cut down everyone in this hut."

Keanuenueokalani gazed at her people, at the mothers with children in their laps, at the men, at ease and unarmed. "They would not stand a chance."

"So what will it be?" Strang demanded. "Do as I want? Or a massacre?"

"Our king would have you hunted down."

Strang laughed. "Neither he nor the council of chiefs knows that the *Poseidon* is in these waters. We can slip away with no one in your government the wiser." He gestured impatiently. "Stop stalling. Tell your mother and father you are staying on board. In fact, tell them we are leaving and will be back to see them in the morning."

"You want to leave now?"

"I don't *want* to. I *am*, and you are coming with me." Strang nodded at her parents. "Tell them, damn it."

Fargo had heard enough. Rising, he hurried around the corner and along the hut to the front. He did not show himself. Drawing the Colt, he waited. Minutes elapsed, and he began to think Strang had changed his mind, when out of the hut came an unhappy bunch of sailors. Muttering and grumbling about being forced to leave, they nonetheless moved toward the shore and the boats. The mates trailed after, urging sluggards along.

The captain was one of the last to emerge, along with his hosts. He had hold of Keanuenueokalani's elbow. "Thank them again for me," he directed. "Tomorrow we will talk more about the ceremony."

Kean began translating.

Fargo chose that moment to slip up behind Strang and jam the Colt's barrel into his spine. "Give me an excuse, any excuse, and I will blow you to hell."

Strang went rigid but otherwise displayed remarkable poise. "Mr. Fargo," he said calmly, without turning his head. "This is an unwelcome development. How did you shed your shackles?"

"Never mind that," Fargo said. Kean's parents could not see the Colt and were staring at him in puzzlement. None of the other Hawaiians had emerged yet, and the sailors were yards away. "I want you to order your men to take the *Poseidon* out to sea."

"What about me?" Strang asked.

"I'm turning you over to the Hawaiian government," Fargo said. Then he would be on the next ship out of Honolulu bound for San Francisco.

"I am afraid I can't allow that."

Fargo gouged the barrel harder. "You can't stop it."

"Oh?" Strang chuckled. "I flatter myself that I am an excellent judge of character. Take yourself, for instance. You do not strike me as the kind to shoot an unarmed

126

man in the back. And so—" Before Fargo could stop him, Strang called out, "Berm! Gliss! Come back here this instant!"

The two mates promptly wheeled and broke into a jog.

"Captain?" Berm said.

"Who is that behind you?" Gliss asked.

Some of the other sailors stopped and looked back.

Fargo was fit to swear. He wanted to shoot Strang. God, how he wanted to shoot him! But Strang was right. He was not the kind to shoot someone in the back. It was a line he had decided long ago he would not cross. Pistol-whipping him, however, was another matter. He raised the Colt to do just that.

"It's Fargo!" Strang bellowed. "Get him! Clap him in irons!"

The first mate and the second mate swapped amazed looks. Berm found his voice first and shouted, "All of you! Get back here! The shanghai is on the loose!"

Fargo swept the Colt down. At the thud Strang staggered but did not fall. Beyond him, sailors were coming on the run. Some had rifles and revolvers. Berm and Gliss each had a pistol but neither had resorted to it.

Fargo was faced with a choice. He could stand and fight and be riddled with slugs, or he could do what he did—namely, shove Strang, seize Keanuenueokalani, and fly around the corner. A shot boomed, and Fargo heard the *thwack* of lead striking the post. Then the hut was between them and the sailors and they fairly flew, Kean displaying remarkable speed despite her long dress.

"Our plan worked!" she beamed. "You have rescued me!"

No, Fargo reflected. All he had done was get her away from Strang, and now the entire crew was after them. He was outnumbered and outgunned. Alone in a strange land, running for his life in the dark of night, he had no cause to celebrate.

They came to the end of the hut. Fargo glanced back and saw moving shadows spill past the front. Several fireflies blossomed, attended by thunder, provoking Strang to roar, "No shooting, you dunderheads! You might hit the girl! I'll keelhaul the man who does!"

Fargo and Keanuenueokalani raced across an open space and on past another hut.

Kean pulled ahead, saying, "I know this land! Let me lead!"

It was fine by Fargo. He held on to her hand as she bounded for the vegetation that fringed the village. Once in among the trees and other plants, they stood a chance of eluding their pursuers. Fifty more feet and they would be there, provided nothing happened.

But something did.

From out of nowhere a pair of burly Hawaiians appeared directly in their path.

17

Fargo brought up the Colt. He did not want to shoot them, but he would be damned if he would let Theodore Strang get hold of him again.

Then Keanuenueokalani said something in Hawaiian and the two men quickly stepped aside.

"Stop them, you clods!" Strang bellowed. "Don't let them get away!"

Neither of the Hawaiians lifted an arm. By their expressions they did not understand English.

Fargo and Kean came to the wall of vegetation and plunged in among the lush trees and plants, Kean moving with a swiftness and surety born of lifelong experience, Fargo relying on her as he seldom relied on anyone when in the wild. She knew the many pathways and could find them in the dark as readily as in the day. They ran flat-out, she in the lead, her warm hand in his.

The sailors were still after them. From behind came shouts and curses and huffing. Strang was bellowing up a storm.

As the minutes went by, the sounds faded. Fargo and Kean were well ahead and in little danger of being caught. Fargo had time to think, and his thoughts were grim. They had escaped but their plight was not much improved. Strang would not be content until he found them. Nearly every sailor would be in on the hunt, and possibly villagers if Strang could convince them to lend a hand. The sailors didn't worry Fargo nearly as much as the Hawaiians. They, like Kean, knew the island, knew it well. They would ferret out every hiding place. Eluding them would prove a challenge.

Kean showed no signs of slowing. Her stamina was remarkable. Fargo had to remember she was a child of nature, not civilization. She was no more at home on a city street than an Apache would be. And like an Apache, she had spent her whole life in the wild, living free, her slender body honed on the whetstone of survival.

Fargo took pride in his own stamina. He could run exceptionally long distances without tiring. But he was puffing some when at long last Kean came to a verdure-covered rise and stopped. She was not breathing heavily at all as she turned to survey their back trail.

Far off toward the village torches flickered, held by men searching for them.

"They will not catch us now," Kean crowed.

"Not tonight, anyway," Fargo amended.

She faced him and, reaching up, tenderly touched his cheek. "Thank you. I am finally shed of Strang and his lust. I am in your debt."

"It was your plan," Fargo noted. "You led us here. I am the one who should be thanking you."

"We will thank each other, then," Kean said, and laughed.

Fargo smiled. He liked this island waif, liked her a lot. "We should push on. They might keep at it all night."

"So? They can never catch us now," Kean declared.

Fargo did not share her confidence. "Maybe not by themselves. But Strang might enlist your people to help."

"My people would never turn on one of their own," Kean said. "They will not help that monster."

"But they don't know he's a monster," Fargo said. "They think you want to marry him of your own free will. In their eyes I am a stranger who took you at gunpoint."

Keanuenueokalani's brow knit. "I had not considered that. Perhaps you are right. If Strang convinces them to

130

aid him, we are in trouble." She paused. "But it might not come to that. My father and mother suspect the truth. Strang forbade me to say anything, and he speaks enough Hawaiian that I had to be careful. But I gave them hints to my true feelings."

"That leaves the rest of your people."

"Remember those two men we passed? I told them that you were my friend, and we were running from a bad white man. They will tell the others."

To Fargo it was a thin thread of hope to rely on, but he did not bring it up. Instead he said, "I leave it up to you. Push on, or find a spot to hole up until daylight." Come to think of it, it might be wiser to get some rest and start the day fresh.

" 'Hole up,' as you call it," Keanuenueokalani said. She tugged on his hand. "Come. I know just the place."

They left the trail and wound through vegetation the likes of which Fargo had never conceived. He did not know what half the plants were. In the dark they were alien shapes, as mysterious as the plant life from another world. Unlike the dank, earthy smell of a Rocky Mountain woodland, here there was a flowery scent, as if Fargo were in a vast garden. In a sense, he supposed, he was, thanks to the riot of wildflowers.

Presently Fargo heard the gurgle of water. Kean brought them to the grassy bank of a stream that flowed out of the mountains and down toward the sea. She headed inland, paralleling the waterway as it climbed ever higher into the interior. After what Fargo judged to be a couple of miles, they rounded a bend and came to a halt.

A loud splashing fell on Fargo's ears. Wet mist dampened his face. He was at the edge of a pool fed by a thirty-foot waterfall. The cascading water glistened in the starlight.

Kean moved around the pool. Without hesitation, she walked into the falling water. Relying on her judgment, Fargo let her lead him under. The sensation was similar to being in a cold, heavy rain. But it only lasted a few seconds. Then they were behind the falls, in a dark, dry nook, ten feet high, about six feet deep, more than enough room for two people.

"I discovered this when I was a young girl," Kean said softly. "It is my special place. I came here often to be alone."

The surface was stone, not earth, as Fargo discovered when he ran a hand over the pitted surface. He mentioned it to Kean.

"Not stone, lava rock. It is said the islands were formed by volcanoes. Lava rock can be found most everywhere."

"The volcanoes aren't still spitting out lava, are they?" To Fargo the notion that anyone would live near an active volcano was downright ridiculous.

"Three of them are, yes. People come from all over to watch the lava bubble and flow. I have gone myself."

"What if the volcano erupts while you are standing next to it?"

Kean shrugged. "I would die. But it would be a beautiful last sight, would it not?"

"If you say so." Fargo never courted an early grave if he could help it. He liked living too much. "I reckon we should get some rest." He sat with his back to the rock wall, his forearms on his knees. "I'll keep watch awhile if you want to sleep."

"There is something else I must do first."

Fargo blinked, and Kean was gone. She had darted out from behind the falls and was swallowed by the night. "Hey!" he called, but she did not answer. He started to rise to go after her but thought better of it. She knew the island; he did not. In the dark he would blunder about like a helpless infant and only get himself lost.

Reluctantly, he sank back down. He leaned back and closed his eyes. God, but he was tired. It had been a long day. The fight on the ship, the swim, and then the long run had tuckered him out.

The sound of the falling water was deceptively peaceful. Fargo felt the tension drain from his sinews. He started to drift off but fought it. He must stay awake until Kean returned. His body, though, would not be denied.

With a start, Fargo snapped awake. He looked about him but Kean was not there. He had the sense he had slept for an hour or more. She should have been back. Alarmed, he went to rise.

The waterfall parted. In a spray of water, Kea-nuenueokalani returned. She shook herself like a tawny cat, then stood smiling down at him in perfect innocence. "Did you miss me?"

"Where have you—" Fargo started to demand and, for one of the few times in his life, was struck speechless. Because it was dark, it had taken a few seconds for what he was seeing to sink in. All he could do was gape.

"Is something the matter?" Kean asked. When he did not answer, she bent toward him. "Say something. Are you hurt or ill?"

"God in heaven," Fargo breathed, more to himself than to her. "What have you gone and done?"

Keanuenueokalani straightened and held her arms out from her sides. "I am me again," she happily declared, spinning in a circle. "Is it not marvelous?"

"Marvelous," Fargo echoed, and meant every syllable.

Gone was the dress. In its place Kean now wore a grass skirt, and *only* a grass skirt. She was naked from the waist up and her feet were bare. Her raven hair, falling past her slender shoulders, reached the swell of her twin mounds. Her breasts were pert perfection, her belly flat and smooth. The grass skirt swished and rustled as, caught up in delight, she spun in another circle.

"I have longed for this moment! This is how I dressed when I was young and carefree, before I was sent to the missionaries and had to wear a dress all the time. Which do you like better? The dress or this?"

Fargo was honest with her. "You can burn the dress if you want. I'll even gather the wood."

Kean giggled girlishly. "I have already torn it to pieces. What is that expression whites have? Ah, yes. I feel as free as a bird."

"You are beautiful," Fargo said.

She did not seem to hear him. "All that talk of wickedness and sin," she bitterly reminisced. "Women must always be clothed from chin to ankles or they are evil and vile. Do you believe that?"

The question caught Fargo off guard. But once again he was honest with her. "I admit I'm more fond of women without their clothes on than with them on."

"See. You agree," Kean said. "Many of my people feel the same. But the missionaries say it is bad, so when they come around, we put on clothes. When they are not around, we dress the old way."

"Don't worry," Fargo assured her, only half in jest. "Your secret is safe with me."

Keanuenueokalani laughed and ran her hands down over her body. "You have no idea how good this feels."

A constriction formed in Fargo's throat and he had to swallow a few times before he could say, "I might have more of an idea than you think."

Kean glanced at the waterfall and inadvertently spoiled the mood by remarking, "I saw torches down the valley. They are still looking for us."

Fargo promptly sobered and rose. "How far off?" he asked, moving to the waterfall. He could see through the watery sheet, but everything on the other side was a blur.

"I am no judge of distance but I would guess a mile or more," Kean imparted. "We are quite safe."

"If you say so." Fargo was not so sure. A competent tracker could trail them by torchlight. It would take considerably longer than by daylight, but it could be done. He had done it himself many times.

"Can you see them?"

Fargo was conscious of the fact she had come up beside him. Her arm brushed his and he could feel the warmth of her luscious body. A tingle ran through him, clear down to his toes.

"Did you hear me?"

"No, I can't," Fargo said, trying in vain to direct his

thoughts away from the pleasurable channels into which they were drifting. There was a time and a place for everything, and this was hardly that time or place.

"I told you we are safe," Keanuenueokalani said. "It must be past ten. We should get some sleep."

Was that all the later it was? Fargo wondered. He figured it should be pushing midnight. "I can try." The truth was, Fargo was not all that tired after his nap. Particularly with the quickening of his pulse from her standing so near that he could smell the flowery fragrance of lilacs, or a flower a lot like them, in her hair.

"I am not tired, either," Kean said. "Maybe it is the excitement of being me again. Or maybe it is something else."

Fargo did not ask what that something else was. On an impulse he thrust his hand into the water, caught a palmful, and tipped the palm to his mouth.

"Are you hungry?" Kean asked. "I know of wild things we can eat."

Fargo had not given any thought to food since he was on the *Poseidon*. Yes, he was famished, but he was averse to having her traipse around in the dark. "I can get by without."

"My mother fed us fish," Kean said, "but I did not eat all that much. Food has not had much taste for me these past months. I have lost a lot of weight."

"It can't be that much." Fargo tried to envision her as plump and couldn't. He turned to sit back down. So did she, at the exact same instant. Only he turned right and she turned left. At the contact of her breasts on his chest, he froze, but not from any sense of embarrassment. He froze because of the hunger the contact kindled, and the heat ignited in his loins.

Keanuenueokalani did not move. She looked up at him, her face sweetly beautiful in the faint starlight that filtered through the thin sheet of water. "Do you feel as I do?"

"How would that be?" Fargo clenched his hands to keep from placing them where he wanted to.

"You know very well," Kean said softly. "I can tell."

"We are on the run. If we want to stay alive, we can't forget that."

"I admire your caution but we are in no danger." Kean raised her hand to his arm. "It has been a long time for me. I would not let Strang touch me. I would not let any of them touch me."

"Women," Fargo said.

"Yes, I am a woman, with a woman's needs. But if you do not want to, that is fine. I understand. You are like the missionaries. You think it is sinful to do and you never do it." Keanuenueokalani wistfully smiled and cupped her breasts. "I will find another man willing to touch me."

"Oh, hell," Skye Fargo said. He knew a lost cause when he felt one.

18

Skye Fargo seldom said no to a willing lady, and it had been his experience that they were often willing at the most unusual moments. Keanuenueokalani was proof. They were being hunted. They were hiding in a niche behind a waterfall. And she was feeling frisky. How loco was that? But since they *were* safe for the time being and it *had* been over a month since he'd savored Molly's charms, the idea of savoring Kean's appealed to him. It certainly appealed to his body. He was rock-hard, with a bulge in his pants that would do justice to a stallion.

Accordingly, when Keanuenueokalani lowered her hands from her breasts, Fargo replaced them with his own. At the contact she arched her back and gave a tiny gasp of delight.

"Oh! I knew you wanted me."

The understatement of the decade. At that instant Fargo wanted her more than he wanted anything. His blood roared in his veins and he was hot all over. His tongue felt thick and that constriction was in his throat again.

"I hope I please you," Kean said.

Fargo hoped she wasn't a talker. Women who gabbed him to death while making love were low on his list of favorite things. He shut her up by covering her wet lips with his while simultaneously squeezing and kneading her firm mounds. She shivered as if cold and cooed like a dove. Her mouth was exquisitely soft. He slid his tongue between her teeth and she sucked on it as she might suck on a piece of pineapple, sending shivers down his spine. She was not prissy, this woman. She went at making love with a hunger that spoke of a healthy appetite.

Fargo was not at all surprised when he felt her fingers pry delicately at his pants. She got his gun belt off and pleased him by carefully lowering it to the ground, unlike some women who just let it drop. Then her fingers were back, working at his pants, and in short order her hand was where she wanted it, fondling his manhood from tip to stem. She knew just what to do and just how to do it. His body throbbed with his need of her.

He pinched both of her nipples and they hardened with yearning. She moaned when he tweaked one, then pulled. His other hand drifted down over her flat belly to her grass skirt. This was a first. Fargo had never made love to a woman in a grass skirt before. He groped for a way of undoing it but could not find a clasp or tie. It occurred to him that the skirt could stay on. All he had to do was part the grass to gain access to her inner charms.

When his hand found her thigh, Kean tilted her head and groaned. Her eyelids were hooded with craving, and there in the pale light, with her bosom full and heaving and her body ripe for touching, she was as lovely a sight as Fargo had ever beheld, and then some.

Their lips fused again in languid kisses that went on and on. No block of wood, this woman. She put all she was into each kiss, her lips seeming to inhale his, her tongue a velvet temptress. She was one of the best kissers he had ever met, and he had kissed a lot of ladies.

Fargo forgot about Strang, about the sailors, about the search for them. He immersed himself in Keanuenueokalani, and in her soft, yielding body. He caressed and stroked and massaged, his hand moving along one smooth leg and then the other, while she squirmed and made little sounds that had no meaning except in the language of raw lust.

Time drifted on clouds of pleasure. Looping an arm around her waist, Fargo gently lowered her onto her back. She shifted under him, saying something about a rock, and then he was on her and the grass skirt rustled as she parted her willowy legs. Her hand on his pole was doing things that brought him to the brink of exploding.

Not yet, he told himself. *Not yet, not yet, not yet.*

Kean's nails found his shoulders and dug deep. Fargo kissed her neck, her ear. He nipped a lobe, sucked on it. He traced his tongue from her throat to her globes and sucked on first one nipple and then the other. She loved it. She gripped his hair and pushed his head against her and whispered soft words in Hawaiian.

Fargo slid a forefinger to her slit. She was wet for him. He parted her nether lips and she glued her upper lips to his. Wetness was everywhere: the wet of her mouth, the wet of her womanhood, the wet mist from the waterfall. He slid his forefinger up into her and was enfolded in more wetness.

She was magnificent. For a few seconds, but only a few, Fargo considered staying with her after he had dealt with Strang. Sunny days of sand and surf and idyllic nights of lovemaking held appeal. But island life was not for him. He was at home in the mountains and prairies; they were in his blood, as much a part of him as his bones and muscles.

The feel of her warm hand cupping him low down jarred Fargo out of his reverie. Now it was his turn to gasp. He had to will himself not to erupt. Inserting a second finger, he pumped in and out, moving his hand ever faster, ever harder. She responded by meeting each stroke with a thrust of her hips. She bit his shoulder, licked his ear.

"Please," she said. "Please."

Fargo obliged. He aligned his member. Then, bit by gradual bit, he fed himself up into her. She shook. She mewed. Looking closer, he was amazed to see tears in her eyes. He thought maybe he was hurting her but that was not the case. They were tears of joy.

"I'll be damned," he blurted.

Their bodies rocked. Their bodies flowed. The lava rock and the waterfall receded into nothingness. There was Fargo and there was the woman under him and that was all. He pumped and pumped, the explosion building, and when Keanuenueokalani gushed and cried out, he could no longer hold back and did the same.

Fargo was a long time floating to earth. He lay cushioned on her breasts, adrift in a delicious daze. Part of him wished he could lie there forever. But his practical side compelled him to roll off her and lie on his back and listen. He heard nothing to indicate their enemies were anywhere near.

"Thank you," Kean said.

Fargo chuckled.

"What?"

"You have that backward," Fargo told her.

"In the old days this was how it was. A woman could lie with a man and feel good about it afterward. She did not feel guilt. She did not feel she was evil." Kean stirred and looked at him. "How can that which is so natural be so wrong?"

"You are asking the wrong person," Fargo answered. He never pretended to have the answers to the why of things. All he knew was what he liked. He figured if he wasn't supposed to like something, he wouldn't have the ability to like it. But since he did, and he did, then he would.

"I wish people did not try to tell other people how to live," Keanuenueokalani said, almost in a whisper. "I am happy being me."

"Makes two of us," Fargo said. His lassitude and the sound of the falling water lulled him to sleep. He dreamed he was riding into an Indian village on the plains. He reined up, and from every lodge emerged a lovely maiden dressed in a grass skirt. They smiled warmly and hurried toward him, their breasts jiggling in the sunlight.

A sharp sound snapped Fargo back to the here and now. He sat up, groping for the Colt, then realized the sound was Kean snoring. He marveled that so small and dainty a nose could make so much noise. He almost pinched it to stop her, but instead found his gun belt and strapped it on.

About to lie back down, Fargo stiffened. Beyond the

waterfall a light flickered in the night. It was a torch, and it was uncomfortably near. Rising in a crouch, he moved to the edge of the falls where the sheet of water was thinnest. He heard voices. Men, speaking Hawaiian.

Fargo glanced at Keanuenueokalani. She had not stirred. He let her sleep and slipped out through the water. The torch was about two hundred yards lower down the slope. Whoever was holding it was winding along the stream, exactly as Fargo and Kean had done. There could be no doubt. A tracker was on their trail, and he would not be alone.

Fargo moved to head them off. He would stop them from reaching the waterfall, and Kean. As soundlessly as a specter he went half the distance, angled into the undergrowth, and crouched. Slicking the Colt from its holster, he waited.

There were two of them, one holding the torch aloft. Both were intent on the soft soil at the edge of the stream.

Stepping into the open, Fargo cocked the Colt. At the click, the Hawaiians stopped and glanced up. Neither, strangely, was armed. They displayed no alarm but regarded him calmly, with a degree of curiosity. The man with the torch said a few words in Hawaiian.

Fargo shook his head to show he did not understand, saying, "I don't savvy." He rose onto his toes to peer behind them. "Where are the rest? Where is Strang and his bunch?"

The two men glanced at each other and then the other man said, "Keanuenueokalani."

"You want to see Kean?" Fargo was suspicious of a trick. If they were working with Strang, then Strang had to be close by. Maybe waiting for him to show them where Kean was so Strang could get his hands on her.

"Keanuenueokalani," the Hawaiian repeated.

"Keanuenueokalani," his companion echoed.

"I can't do that," Fargo told them. "Not until I'm sure it is safe."

The man bearing the torch came toward him. Instantly, Fargo pointed the Colt. "That's far enough."

141

If his warning was not clear, brandishing the Colt was. The man stopped and addressed him in Hawaiian, which might as well be Latin as far as Fargo was concerned.

"Keanuenueokalani," the man ended his appeal.

Fargo tried again. "Stay where you are." He motioned to stress his meaning and backed toward the waterfall, only to have them follow him. They did not act hostile but he could not take the gamble. A third time he gestured and backed away. Two steps he took, and a hard object was jabbed into the small of his back. A click revealed he was not the only one with a gun.

"Twitch and you die, landlubber."

"Wells?" Fargo wanted to kick himself. He had been so intent on the trackers and on who might be behind them that he never thought to check behind himself.

"None other." The sailor chuckled. "Me and a friend."

A hand extended past Fargo's elbow and gripped the Colt. "I would let go, were I you," advised the second sailor. "The captain wants you alive, but he gave his consent to do whatever we need to if you act up."

Angry at his lapse, Fargo relinquished the Colt. "The four of you can pat yourselves on the back."

"Four?" Wells said, and laughed. "Oh. No. You've got it wrong, mister. Those lunkheads are here on their own account."

"How is that?"

"The girl's father sent them to find her. Captain Strang overheard, and had us tag along without the Hawaiians catching on. When you popped out of nowhere, we were tickled as could be." Wells poked Fargo with the revolver. "Let's get this over with. Where is she?"

"I wouldn't know."

Fargo never saw the blow that felled him. He dropped to his knees and swayed, struggling to stay conscious.

"There is more where that came from," Wells said. "A lot more. Now I will ask you again. Where is the captain's woman?"

"She knows this island, every path and hiding place. I don't. I knew I would only slow her down so I told her to go on ahead." Fargo congratulated himself. It sounded believable.

"Some idiots never learn," Wells said, and hiked his revolver to hit him again.

"She went on alone," Fargo insisted. "She said something about going to the next village for help."

Afflicted by uncertainty, Wells hesitated.

"Maybe he's telling the truth," the other sailor threw in. "It wouldn't take her more than two days on foot. She could be back in four with a small army."

"The captain wouldn't like that," Wells said.

"No, he sure wouldn't," his friend agreed. "Maybe we should get word to him right away."

"The captain told us not to come back without the girl, remember? We go empty-handed and he will be mad. Do you want that? You know how he is when he is mad."

"I sure do," the other said. "But we'll take the land-lubber with us so he can hear it from the landlubber's own mouth. That way he will be mad at the landlubber, not at us."

Wells brightened and wagged his weapon. "That's genius, Seth. Pure genius. I would love to see Strang break this landlubber over his knee. After all the trouble he's caused us, he deserves it."

"Then we have an accord?" Seth asked.

"Indeed, we do." Wells bobbed his head at the Hawaiians. "But what about those two? The captain didn't tell us what to do with them."

"Then we are free to do whatever we want," Seth proposed. "I say we put a bullet in each of their simple heads and leave them for the worms."

"You're just full of genius notions," Wells complimented him.

While they were debating, Fargo inched his hand toward his ankle and the Arkansas toothpick.

The Hawaiians, unable to speak English, were content to stand and stare. The man with the torch even smiled when Wells turned toward him and raised the pistol.

"Look at 'em. The dolts. They make it too easy, like shooting rabbits or ducks."

"Dumb as a stump," his partner concurred. "Kill them and let's be on our way."

At that instant, Fargo's hand found the toothpick.

19

Fargo drew the toothpick as he spun. Wells was aiming a Smith & Wesson at one of the Hawaiians. The other sailor held the Colt and also had a knife in a leather sheath at his hip.

Fargo drove the double-edged blade up and in. The toothpick sliced as easily into Wells's gut as a butcher knife into pudding. Wells bleated and jerked back, which was the last thing he should have done. Warm blood gushed in a scarlet geyser, some of it spattering Fargo's face and buckskin shirt.

"Damn you!" Wells shrieked, and went to train the Remington on him.

Already rising, Fargo stabbed him again, this time in the torso. He felt the blade glance off a rib, felt it scrape and then the spongy sensation of steel shearing through internal organs.

Wells screamed.

At the same instant Fargo grabbed for the Colt, but as he wrested it free, he was struck a blow to the temple that staggered him and the Colt slipped from his grasp.

"You don't do that to my mate, you bastard!" the other sailor raged as he whipped out his long knife. Crouching, he circled, wary of the toothpick.

Fargo's ear was ringing. Gritting his teeth against the pain, he feinted, sidestepped, and lanced his blade at the sailor's chest. The man skipped aside. The whole while, Fargo was acutely aware that Wells was to one side of them and might shoot him at any moment. He had to deal with this one quickly.

But the man was crafty, and he was adept with his knife. He held it close to his chest, his arm cocked, ready to parry or stab. He was confident, too, and wore a mocking smile. "I should thank you, landlubber," he taunted. "The captain can't blame me for killing you, not after what you did to Wells." Still smiling, he weaved right, then left, and struck.

Fargo countered. Steel rang on steel. The sailor's blade was longer than his, and thicker. He had to watch that he did not lose fingers. He speared the toothpick high, going for the man's throat, but again the sailor expertly dodged.

"Not bad, landlubber, but not good enough, either. I've been in plenty of knife fights and have yet to meet my match."

Fargo believed him. He had been in plenty of knife fights, too, and he knew skill when he saw it. He narrowly evaded a swing at his neck that would have nearly decapitated him and retaliated with a sweep at the sailor's midriff that was adroitly avoided. Damn, this one was good! It did not help matters that Fargo dearly wanted to tear his gaze away and see where Wells had gotten to. He was surprised Wells had not shot him yet and wondered if the two Hawaiians had taken a hand.

Then Fargo had no time for thought as the sailor closed. Fargo was hard-pressed to counter. They were in perpetual motion, a graceful dance that belied the deadly intent.

The only way for Fargo to prevail was to take a chance. He took it. He stabbed, extending his arm farther than he should, an amateur's mistake, and, pretending to slip, he bent at the knee.

The sailor took the bait. Grinning, thinking his opportunity had come, he drove his long knife at Fargo's heart. His amazement at the result was understandable. Instead of burying his blade in Fargo, he gaped at the toothpick embedded to the hilt in his own chest and blurted the last words he would utter, "This can't be!"

Life faded, the sailor collapsed, and Fargo, yanking the Arkansas toothpick out, whirled and sought his other enemy. He need not have worried. Not because the Hawaiians had helped, because they were still standing exactly where they had been when the fight began. No, he need not have worried because Wells was on his back, dead, his face a twisted mask.

"Skye! Skye! Are you all right?" Keanuenueokalani came running out of the night. She took one look at the dead sailors and threw herself into Fargo's arms. "I thought I heard voices! And you were gone."

Her skin and lips were so wonderfully warm and soft that Fargo had to force himself to step back and nod at the pair of trackers. "Your father sent them. Strang sent these other two to follow them."

Kean and the pair spoke in rapid-fire Hawaiian. Her reaction spoke volumes. When they were done, she excitedly translated. "We must go back. My father has realized his mistake. He wants to help us."

"Are you sure you can trust these two?" Fargo asked while wiping the toothpick clean on Wells's shirt.

"Strang has revealed his true nature. He accused my father and mother of deceiving him, of playing him for a fool, as you whites would say. He hit my father and slapped my mother and demanded to know where I had gone. He did not believe them when they told him they did not know."

Fargo sheathed the toothpick. He picked up the Colt and the Smith & Wesson, and holstered the former while tucking the latter under his belt.

"Didn't you hear me?" Kean asked. "We have a chance now. My people will rise up and drive the sailors back to their ship."

Fargo was still not convinced. "What about the debt your father owes Strang for saving his life?"

"It was wiped away when Strang hit him. Among my people, for one man to strike another is the worst of insults. According to the old ways, the only way to erase such an insult is in blood."

The two trackers were looking at them expectantly, awaiting their decision.

Fargo nodded. "All right. We'll go." If what she said was true, her people would need his help as much as he needed theirs. Knives and clubs and fish spears were no match for guns. There were more Hawaiians than there were sailors, but the rifles and revolvers of the seamen would quickly blast the hell out of the Hawaiians.

Keanuenueokalani relayed the news to the trackers, who turned without comment and started back. She tugged at Fargo's arm, saying, "If we hurry we can reach my village before dawn."

Shortly before, as it turned out.

Fargo was winded and in dire need of rest. But it was not to be. They crouched in the verdant vegetation a spear's toss from the huts and took stock. The tracker with the torch had put it out well before they got there, and now, pointing with it, he whispered something in Hawaiian.

"He asks if you see the sentry," Kean translated.

A sailor with a rifle was making a circuit of the village. A sentry, and he was not the only one. Fargo spied two others. Strang was thorough, as usual.

"We must let my father know we are here," Keanuenueokalani said. "I will sneak to his hut. Wait for me."

"Nothing doing."

"Please," Kean said, placing her hand on his. "I will be careful. Dressed as I am, the sailors might not recognize me if they see me. They will think I am just another woman."

Fargo did not like the idea, but he relented. He regretted it as the minutes crawled by and she did not reappear. The two Hawaiians might as well be statues, but he could not stop shifting his weight from one leg to the other and glancing to the east where the horizon had grown lighter than the rest of the dark vault of sky. Daybreak was not far off.

Then two figures appeared, darting from hut to hut. Keanuenueokalani and her father, shadows among the shadows. They waited until the sentry had his back to them and made it into the greenery without being spotted.

"About time," Fargo grumbled.

Imaikalani whispered to his daughter. After he was done, Kean turned. "He says that he is glad to meet you. He thanks you for looking after me and asks if we can count on your help when we wage war against the men from the sea."

"The question is," Fargo responded, "can I count on him?"

Daughter and father whispered a while. "He says that you can. He says that he was never happy about giving me to Captain Strang, but Strang saved his life. To you that is a strange thing for him to do, but to my father it was a matter of honor. Honor according to the old ways, not the new ways of the missionaries. My father likes the old ways better. They are the ways of the warrior and not of those who turn the other cheek."

"Tell your father I understand," Fargo said when she paused.

"There is more. My father says Strang is not the man my father thought he was. Strang showed his true nature after you took me. He hit my father when my father refused to hunt for us until daylight. He grabbed my mother by the throat when she came between them. His men beat some of our men when they tried to help."

Fargo was surprised Strang had lost control. But then, Strang was obsessed with Keanuenueokalani, and with power. Deprive him of the one and he would exercise the other.

"My father cannot forgive such treatment. Our people will not stand the insult. When Captain Strang returns in the morning, we are going to drive him into the sea or die trying."

Fargo glanced across the lagoon. The *Poseidon* was lit from stem to stern. So was the water for a score of yards around the ship, a safeguard against attack. It made sense for the Hawaiians to wait for the sailors to come to them and not be decimated in a vain bid to board the vessel.

"My father has sent men to spread word. Everyone knows their part. As soon as the fighting starts, the women will take the children to safety. My father says—"

Fargo reached out and covered Kean's mouth. The sentry was coming toward them. The sailor was between the huts and the vegetation, the rifle across his shoulder as a soldier would carry it, whistling a sea shanty. One of the trackers started to rise but Kean's father whispered and the man sank back down. Oblivious to their presence, the sentry went past and was soon lost to view.

"So will you help us?" Kean wanted to be assured.

"Yes," Fargo said. "But I want to know how your father plans to go about waging his war."

She put the question to Imaikalani and relayed his answer. "As soon as the boats from the ship touch the sand, my father will lead the warriors in a rush from the huts."

"That is what I was afraid he had in mind," Fargo said. "Strang will be expecting something like that. His men will cut your warriors down before they can get close enough to use their weapons."

Once more Kean translated. "My fathers says there is wisdom in your words. He asks what you would do."

Fargo had been giving it some thought. He outlined his idea.

Smiling and nodding, Kean said, "It might work. But you will be taking a terrible risk. I must take part, too."

"No."

"Why not? Because I might be hurt? Have you forgotten that all this is over me? Since I am the cause of the blood that will be spilled, it is only right that I be involved."

"No," Fargo said again. "Strang is to blame, not you. I won't let you take part."

"You cannot stop me," Kean said, adding indignantly, "I am a grown woman. I can do as I will." She turned

150

to her father. Their exchange resulted in, "My father agrees. If I am there, Strang will be less likely to suspect we are up to something."

She had a point but Fargo still balked. "You will be in the open. You could take a stray slug."

"What sort of person would I be if I let the men of my village die for me but did not risk my own life?" Keanuenueokalani asked. "It is settled. As you say, what will be, will be."

Fargo looked at her father, who smiled. "Did you tell him I am against it?"

"No."

"Tell him."

"No."

Fargo pointed at Kean and then at the beach, and shook his head. Imaikalani's knit brow and wag of his head showed he did not understand. "Damn it, Kean. Ask him to keep you out of it as a favor to me."

"My mind is made up. Besides, I told him you think it is a wonderful idea."

"What kind of father lets his flesh and blood be shot to ribbons?"

"You exaggerate," Kean countered. "Strang will not harm me, nor will he let any of his men harm me."

Fargo compressed his lips into a thin line. He could argue until doomsday and she would not give in. "You think you are clever, don't you?"

"And you think you are the only one who has the right to vengeance," Keanuenueokalani said fiercely.

"No, I don't," Fargo said, but she wasn't listening.

"I was the one taken from my home, from my family, from my people. I was the one held captive on the ship for weeks on end. I was put in leg irons the same as you. Surely I, too, am entitled to revenge?"

Fargo wanted to say she wasn't, but he could not look her in the eyes and lie. "You are as entitled as I am," he admitted.

"More so," Kean said.

They were running out of time. The eastern sky was brightening.

"All right. Have it your way. But stay close to me, and when the shooting starts, hug the ground and stay down until it is over."

Keanuenueokalani smiled sweetly and placed her hand on his shoulder. "I am yours to command."

"Women," Fargo muttered.

Imaikalani stirred and said something to Kean.

"My father says it is time to carry out your plan. He vows that before this day is done, either Strang and the other whites will be gone or we will."

"By gone he means dead."

"Yes. What else?"

"That is what I am afraid of," Skye Fargo said.

20

Fargo decided to take the sentry when the man made his next pass between the huts and the vegetation. Easing onto his belly, Fargo crawled to the edge of the growth and drew the toothpick.

Presently the sailor came strolling back, whistling to himself. Fargo did not like that. The other sentries might wonder if the whistling abruptly stopped.

Then the sailor halted, yawned loudly, shifted his rifle from one arm to the other, and stretched. He shook his head to keep awake and gazed to the east, apparently eager for dawn to break and his sentry duty to be over.

Fargo launched himself from the undergrowth. He made no noise so it must have been some sixth sense that warned the man, because he spun and brought up the rifle. It was not quite level when Fargo sheared the toothpick into soft flesh just below the sternum, sheared it up and in so the tip pierced the sailor's heart.

The man grunted. That was all. Blood dribbling from both corners of his mouth, he melted to the earth, lay twitching, and was still. No sooner did the twitching stop than the two Hawaiians who had tracked Fargo glided out of hiding, seized hold of either arm, and dragged the dead man off. When they reappeared, Keanuenueokalani and Imaikalani were with them, and her father had the rifle. One of the trackers had the dead sailor's clothes.

"Does he know how to shoot?" Fargo whispered.

She put the question to Imaikalani. "He says that he has seen white men do it."

"Tell him we must do this quietly," Fargo advised.

"He understands."

The other two sentries were between the huts and the water. One patrolled the strip of beach, the other was nearer the village. They posed a problem in that they were nearly always in sight of one another. Jump one and the other was bound to see and shout to the ship.

Crouched beside a hut, Fargo consulted with the chief through Kean. Imaikalani had an idea. He sent one of the trackers to bring a dozen warriors. Instructions were imparted. Four hastened to the west end of the village, and from there slipped into the sea. Neither sentry noticed.

They were seals in the water, these islanders. They swam superbly, covering more distance underwater than Fargo ever could, rising with only their noses and mouths briefly visible and then submerging again until they were near the sentry patrolling the beach.

Now came the crucial part. Other warriors were ready to jump the sailor near the huts. But their timing had to be perfect or one or the other would yell for help.

Imaikalani solved that problem. He rose and boldly strode toward the nearest sentry, smiling and talking in Hawaiian.

The man had a revolver tucked under his belt and started to draw it. "Hold it right there." He blinked in surprise. "Oh, it's you, Chief. What do you want? Strang said you are supposed to stay in your hut." He motioned for Imaikalani to stop.

The chief kept on coming, kept on smiling. He pointed at the *Poseidon* and spoke.

The sentry glanced at the ship, then held out an arm. "That's far enough. Don't you speak any English? Go back to your hut."

Imaikalani waved an arm toward the ship. Or so it seemed to the sentry. In reality it was a signal to the four in the water, who by now were close to shore and the other sentry on the beach.

The man had seen Imaikalani and had turned to watch, his back to the water. He heard the four men rise dripping out of the sea, but before he could bring his weapon to bear, they were on him. Four knives stabbed home. They caught him before he fell.

At that instant the chief grabbed the wrists of the sentry, trying to make him return to his hut. Startled, the man opened his mouth to cry out but the other Hawaiians were on him in a rush, smothering him with a hand over his mouth as well as their numbers. He was still alive when they bore him to the ground, but he was not breathing when they picked him up and hastened toward a hut to hide the body.

"My father handled that well," Keanuenueokalani said proudly.

Fargo thought so, too. Luck had been with them in that the lookout had not seen them. Or maybe he had dozed off.

They had to move quickly.

Word had spread throughout the village. At the chief's command, warriors filled the huts near the shore while the women and children were hurried to huts farther back. Three Hawaiians with builds similar to the slain sailors' emerged dressed in their clothes and accompanied Fargo, Kean, and her father to the beach. There, Fargo and Kean stood with their hands behind their backs, as if bound, Fargo first shifting his gun belt so the Colt was not visible from the ship.

"I pray this works," Keanuenueokalani said, her head bowed.

"Even if it does," Fargo responded, "some of your people are bound to die." He was not trying to upset her; he was merely stating a fact.

"I know," Kean said sadly. "Yet another reason I must take part. I could not ask my people to risk their lives on my behalf and not risk my own."

Her father said something to her, and laughed, and

Kean managed a smile. "He says this is like the old days. He misses those times. We were a happy people then. We lived in harmony with the sea and the land, and were content."

"You can be that way again," Fargo said.

"No, we cannot. Our old life is gone forever. Even our king has said so, although he had brought back a few of the old ways to—" Kean stopped. "What is that?"

A commotion had broken out on the ship. Voices were raised and figures were moving about.

"The lookout or someone else has noticed us," Fargo guessed. "It won't be long now."

It wasn't. Barely two minutes went by and Captain Strang's deep voice boomed across the water. "Ho, there! Keach! They have been caught?"

The question was addressed to one of the dead sailors. Fargo answered in the man's stead, hollering, "You have eyes, don't you? How long are we supposed to stand here waiting? Wells tied the rope so tight I can't feel my hands." He knew it was a mistake the moment he said it, but the harm had been done.

"Where is Wells?" came the surly question.

"Getting a bite to eat," Fargo shouted.

A laugh rolled in with the surf. "Sharks have to eat, too, as you will shortly find out."

The three boats were lowered. It appeared to Fargo that nearly every last seaman was coming ashore. Strang stood in the bow of the foremost, his brawny arms folded across his broad chest. Berm was in the bow of the second, Gliss in the bow of the third.

"Row, you sluggards! Put your backs to those oars!"

Keanuenueokalani watched the approaching boats with trepidation. "This is it."

"Soon," Fargo said, marking their progress.

"I want to thank you for all you have done for me," Kean said softly, "in case I don't get to later."

"Remember to drop flat," Fargo reminded her. He placed his right hand on the Colt.

To the east a golden crown framed the world's rim. Out on the lagoon, the oars of the three boats rose and

156

fell in practiced cadence. Strang was staring at Fargo and Keanuenueokalani. Or was he? Fargo wondered. Maybe Strang's suspicion had been aroused and he was studying the Hawaiians who were pretending to be sailors. To divert his attention, Fargo shouted, "What now, Strang? Do you make me walk the plank?"

"That sort of thing went out with Blackbeard," was the reply. "No, I have something better in mind for you."

"Care to share what it is?" Fargo prompted.

"Remember those sharks I mentioned?" Strang and many of his men laughed.

That was when Keanuenueokalani called out, "It is not too late to change your mind, Theodore. Turn around. Go back to your ship and leave us in peace."

The boats were close enough that Strang did not need to shout. "You jest, my dear. Why would I give up when my dream is about to come true? In a very short while, you will be mine for all time."

"Didn't my running away teach you anything? I don't want to marry you, Theodore. I never have."

"Your feelings are irrelevant," Strang smugly informed her. "Besides, give yourself six months and you will change your mind. You will come to accept me and enjoy your new lot in life."

"Never!" Kean cried, and in the emotion of the moment she forgot herself, forgot she was to keep her arms behind her back as if they were tied. Taking a step, she shook her fist at him. "Never! Do you hear me?"

By then the boats were barely twenty feet out. Strang stiffened and lowered his arms, saying, "I thought you were bound." He glanced at Fargo, then at Imaikalani, and finally at the Hawaiians dressed as sailors. In the space of a heartbeat he divined the truth.

"To arms! To arms! It's a trap!"

The sailors were slow to react. They thought everything was under control. As they grabbed for rifles and revolvers another shout pierced the dawn, this one from Imaikalani.

At his cry warriors poured from the huts bordering the beach.

Fargo did not wait for Kean to drop flat as he had instructed. Whirling, he seized her by the shoulders, hooked a foot behind her legs, and took her down, careful not to hurt her in the process.

Imaikalani and the three Hawaiians dressed as sailors dived, too, but not to the ground. In long bounds they plunged into the surf. Her father and two others made it under. The last man was not as fortunate. The blast of a rifle blew out the rear of his skull.

Fargo snapped a shot at a sailor with a rifle and the sailor clutched his side and fell. But no one fired at him. The rest were taking aim at the swarm of onrushing warriors.

"Steady, boys, steady!" Captain Strang bawled. "Wait for my command and make every shot count!"

The wave of Hawaiians was almost to the waves lapping the beach. Fargo aimed at Strang, thinking to end the battle before it began by ending the life of the one person responsible, but as he went to shoot, Strang ducked to avoid a hastily hurled spear. The next second, by the deft use of their oars, the sailors in Strang's boat began to swing the boat broadside.

Fargo had let go of Keanuenueokalani. He regretted it when she surged to her feet and joined the charge.

None of the Hawaiians were whooping and yipping, as mainland warriors were wont to do. In grim silence, save for the splashing of their swarthy bodies, they hurled themselves at the boats—and were met by a thunderous volley.

It was as Fargo had feared it would be, a slaughter, with five or six falling. The sailors in the other boats opened up, adding to the din, and more Hawaiians fell. But then the warriors were at the boats, stabbing and thrusting and clubbing. A brutal melee ensued, horrific in its savagery, the sailors outnumbered but able to momentarily hold their own thanks to their guns.

The blasts of rifles and revolvers, the shrieks and screams of the wounded and the dying, and the lusty oaths of the seamen rose in a chaos of bloodletting.

Fargo pushed erect. Both sides had forgotten him in

the frenzied extremity of combat. The water rose as high as his ankles and then his knees. All he needed was one clear shot, but the mad whirl of battle prevented him from catching more than a glimpse of Strang.

Guns were still going off, but in fewer numbers as sailors emptied their firearms and were unable to take the time to reload. Knife, club, and spear were being used to deadly effect. Blood by the gallon spilled into the lagoon, turning the clear water a murky scarlet.

Above the bedlam rose Strang's roar. "Away the boats! Back to the ship or we are done for!"

Bodies dotted the surf, some floating and still, others thrashing in their death throes. The boats were turning but with awful slowness. Most of the sailors could ill afford to take their eyes off the press of Hawaiians to bend to the oars.

Fargo saw a seaman sight down a rifle at Keanuenueokalani. He was quicker; his shot took the top of the man's head off.

Suddenly Theodore Strang reared above a knot of furiously fighting warriors at the bow. A knife flashed as he laid about him in a berserk fury. Two, three, four Hawaiians fell. Strang raised his arm to dispatch a fifth but the blow never landed. From out of the mayhem flew a spear. The tip caught Strang at the base of the throat and lanced through his neck.

Strang dropped his knife and grabbed the spear as his life's blood spewed in a geyser. He looked about him and his eyes alighted on Keanuenueokalani. A red hand extended toward her. The fingers opened. Then, like a great tree cut off at the roots, Captain Theodore Strang pitched over the side.

Ironically, only then did the sailors succeed in turning the boat, and they rowed like madmen for the *Poseidon*. The other boats were not long in following.

As for the Hawaiians, those still able helped the wounded and the dying to shore. At a shout from Imaikalani the women raced from the village to help, many of the children tagging along.

A great weariness came over Fargo. He stood and

watched the sailors as they clambered on board and raised anchor. They had had enough. The *Poseidon* was leaving without her master.

A warm hand slipped into his. "In a day or two we can take you to Honolulu if you want," Keanuenueokalani said. Her whole body was spattered with red drops. "There you can book passage on the next ship to San Francisco."

Fargo gazed at her bare breasts and shapely legs. "There is no hurry," he assured her. "No hurry at all."

LOOKING FORWARD!
The following is the opening
section from the next novel in the exciting
Trailsman **series from Signet:**

THE TRAILSMAN #313
TEXAS TIMBER WAR

The piney woods of East Texas, 1860—
where danger for the Trailsman
lurks in the forest thickets.

The big man in buckskins raced his horse along the bank
of the bayou. The area was thickly wooded, so the magnificent Ovaro stallion had to weave around and through
clumps of loblolly pines and cypress trees. Even though
the sun was shining overhead, the forest canopy ensured
that this part of eastern Texas remained in perpetual
shadow.

Skye Fargo's lake blue eyes narrowed as he heard the
rattle of more gunshots. The shooting had started a couple of minutes earlier as he made his way through the
area, and the swift urgency of the reports told Fargo
that trouble had erupted somewhere in front of him.

Some parts of this forest were all but impenetrable,
and as Fargo reined his black-and-white mount to a halt

and listened to the gunfire, he considered staying out of it for a change. Whatever was going on, he might not be able to reach the spot in time to help anyone.

But that thought had been fleeting. Fargo wasn't the sort of man to ignore someone else's danger. Moving as fast as possible, he headed in the direction of the shots.

By the time he reached the bayou, though, the gunfire had shifted. The shots now came from somewhere upstream. Fargo turned the Ovaro to follow them.

As he rode, he became aware of another sound—a deep, throaty *chug-chug-chug* that he recognized as the noise of a steam engine. He reined the Ovaro around a bend and came in sight of a stern-wheeled riverboat churning through the waters of the bayou.

Men in canoes paddled after the riverboat, and other men who ran along the banks peppered the vessel with rifle fire. A few puffs of powder smoke from the riverboat told Fargo that someone on board was trying to put up a fight, but they weren't mustering much of one.

The attackers had to be river pirates, Fargo thought. No one else would have any reason to try to stop the boat by force like that.

He reached for the Henry rifle that jutted from a sheath strapped to the Ovaro's saddle. Fargo cranked the repeater's loading lever as he brought the rifle to his shoulder. Three canoes pursued the riverboat, and Fargo aimed at the waterline of the one closest to the vessel. He sent a couple of bullets smashing through the canoe's hull just below the surface of the bayou, then shifted his aim to the second canoe.

The men in the first canoe barely had time to realize what had happened before Fargo drilled the second canoe as well. Both of the little craft began taking on water. With yells of alarm, the pirates abandoned their pursuit of the riverboat and turned to wave their arms and point at Fargo. The men paddling the third canoe dropped their paddles and picked up rifles. They started firing at the big man on the black-and-white horse.

So did the men on the banks of the bayou. As the riverboat chugged on around another bend, the pirates turned their attention to the man who had interrupted their attack. Shots blasted out, further shattering what had been the peaceful stillness of the piney woods, and Fargo heard bullets ripping through the air around his head.

He had shot holes in the canoes, instead of in the men paddling them, because he didn't know all the details of what was going on here and didn't want to kill anybody needlessly. Also, shooting somebody who wasn't even aware of his presence went against the grain for Fargo.

But now they were trying to kill him, so all restraints were off. Fargo's Henry cracked swiftly and mercilessly. One of the men in the third canoe toppled out of the little craft, landing in the bayou with a great splash of murky water. A man on the near bank fell as well, also ventilated by a slug from Fargo's rifle. A third man clutched a bullet-shattered shoulder and howled in pain.

Even though the pirates outnumbered Fargo by more than twelve to one, his deadly accurate fire must have unnerved them. The men on the far bank bolted for cover, disappearing into the trees. So did the ones on the nearer bank. And the men in the canoes paddled hard for the opposite shore, giving up the fight.

The two canoes Fargo had holed sank before they got there, with the men inside them floundering into the water and swimming for the bank. The frantic desperation of their thrashing reminded Fargo that alligators lurked in many of these East Texas streams.

Fargo held his fire and let the men flee. The canoe that was still afloat reached the shore, and the men inside it leaped out and dragged the craft onto the bank. The swimmers clambered out of the bayou and joined them. They all vanished quickly, because they had to take only a few steps before the thicket swallowed them up.

Fargo reined the Ovaro away from the bank and

moved back into the woods, not wanting to leave himself exposed to any bushwhackers' bullets. He brought the stallion to a halt and sat there listening, an intent expression on his ruggedly handsome face with its close-cropped dark beard. The forest was quiet. All the shooting had spooked the birds and small animals and made them fall silent.

When Fargo was satisfied that the pirates had fled, rather than doubling back to try to jump him, he slid the Henry in the saddle sheath and hitched the Ovaro into motion again.

A few minutes later he hit the trail he had been following earlier, before leaving it to seek out the source of the gunfire. The trail ran west out of Louisiana toward the settlement of Jefferson, roughly paralleling Big Cypress Bayou. But since the trail twisted and turned due to the varying thickness of the forest, and the bayou followed an equally meandering path, sometimes they were within sight of each other and sometimes they weren't.

As the broad, slow-moving stream came into view again, Fargo was surprised to see that the riverboat had pulled in close to the bank and come to a halt. It had to be bound for Jefferson, which was still several miles away, Fargo reckoned. The big paddlewheel at the rear of the boat had stopped turning, but smoke rose from the twin stacks, showing that the engine still had steam up.

Fargo cut across a field dotted with pine and cypress to reach the bayou. His keen eyes scanned the decks and didn't see anyone moving around. Crates were stacked on the main deck, goods bound for Jefferson, no doubt.

The steamboats that plied these waters came up the Mississippi River from New Orleans and veered off into the Red River north of Baton Rouge, then followed the Red to Shreveport, Louisiana. From Shreveport the boats steamed up Big Cypress Bayou to sprawling

Caddo Lake, which straddled the border between Louisiana and Texas, and according to local legend, had been formed by the tremendous earthquake that had shaken the whole middle part of the country nearly fifty years earlier.

Beyond Caddo Lake, Big Cypress Bayou continued to flow westward and took the paddlewheelers all the way to Jefferson. That was as far into Texas as the river traffic could penetrate, but it was far enough to open up all of eastern Texas to the rest of the world.

As a result, Jefferson wasn't the backwoods settlement it might have been otherwise, but rather a sophisticated, fast-growing city that rivaled Galveston in importance as Texas's second-largest port.

The flow of commerce wasn't all one way, either. Numerous cotton plantations were located in the area, and in the past decade, logging operations had moved in as well to harvest the riches of the hardwood forests. On the return trips, the riverboats that came to Jefferson were loaded with bales of cotton and stacks of timber. At first the loggers had tried floating the felled trees down the bayou, but the current was so slow that this proved to be impractical. Riverboats had turned out to be the answer.

Fargo was well aware of all this, his fiddlefooted ways having taken him through the region several times in the past. He knew this riverboat wouldn't have stopped along here unless something else was wrong, so he swung down from the saddle and looped the reins around the horn. The Ovaro was well trained and would stay put.

"Hello the boat!" Fargo called in his deep, powerful voice. "Permission to come aboard?"

He gathered his muscles to make the leap from the bank to the deck.

Instead he jumped backward as a shot rang out and a bullet smacked into the bank ahead of him.

"Permission denied!" a man's voice bellowed.

The voice and the shot both came from the thicket of crates on the main deck. Fargo's hand dropped instinctively to the butt of the big Colt revolver holstered on his right hip, but he left the gun where it was since he couldn't see anybody to shoot at. Anyway, he figured that had been a warning shot, rather than one intended to hit him.

"Hold your fire, damn it!" he said. "I don't mean you any harm." A grim smile tugged at his mouth. "Fact of the matter is, I'm the hombre who chased off those pirates who were trying to board you, back down the bayou."

A man emerged from behind the pile of cargo, carrying a rifle. "That so?" he asked. The thick wooden peg that replaced his left leg from the knee down made a clumping sound on the deck as he moved. He was tall and scrawny, with a gray spade beard and a battered old riverman's cap crammed down on a bald head. He went on, "What the hell business was it of yours, anyway?"

"It looked to me like you folks were in trouble, so I decided to help," Fargo replied. "Simple as that. Just like I figure something else is wrong now, or you wouldn't have stopped here. You'd have gone on and made port in Jefferson."

"Got it all figured out, ain't you?" The man spat into the bayou but kept the rifle trained on Fargo. "What's your name, mister?"

"Skye Fargo."

The gaunt old-timer's eyes widened in recognition. "I heard of you," he said. "You're the fella they call the Trailsman."

"Sometimes," Fargo admitted.

No other series packs this much heat!

THE TRAILSMAN

**Available wherever books are sold or at
penguin.com**